She Only Boots For Me

ALEXANDER KING

Also by Alexander King

It Looks Like You're Writing a Letter

ISBN: 978-0-9931359-1-0

For Marlowe

ACKNOWLEDGMENTS

Lucy for her continued love and support, and for being the first 'beta tester'. Andy Curry for also beta testing, and designing the book cover.

"The ultimate hidden truth of the world, is that it is something that we make, and could just as easily make differently."

- *David Graeber*

1

Jimmy's body slammed against the bar back. A shower of smart cocktails continued to cycle through their hues as they dripped down the wall behind him.

"Come on now Clive," he shouted from the relative safety of the puddle of stale synthohol, "we just want to look in the cellar, man!"

"Not fuckin' likely Jimmy you weasel!" screamed Clive as he prowled his realistic recreation of a 1980s English pub. Despite the damage he was currently wreaking on it, Clive was proud of his little slice of a country and time he never personally knew. He fired another blast of stun pellets into the imitation wood of the bar.

"But Clive!" pleaded Jimmy, "I thought we were pals?"

"Pals?" snorted Clive, "You're a fuckin' copper, how could we be friends? You beady eyed little fucker."

Jimmy spent another choice few moments wishing he was armed, something he did reasonably regularly. A little help would be good right now.

"Davonne? You out there?" he shouted. His partner - albeit only of three months - was somewhere else in the pub but had remained somewhat subdued as soon as everything kicked off.

"I'm going to call for backup," said a faint voice from an opposite corner.

"We can handle this Davonne, this is just a little misunderstanding, that's all."

"Misunderstanding my arse," bellowed Clive through a plume of spittle. "You and your fat arsed partner called me a crook, and you know I'm straight as a die!"

Jimmy shrugged, he had a point. But in their defence, Clive was a drug dealer and did have around 30 Chinese immigrants locked up in his cellar. "Clive, think about how much money I've put over this bar. We can clear this up! Haven't I always been straight with you?"

"Straight my arse. Come out from behind there, let me shoot you, then fuck off."

It appeared that diplomacy may not win the day here, and Davonne was less than useless. They'd have a chat about this later, Jimmy thought. A nice chat. In the meantime, Jimmy was buttoning up his leather trench coat and securing his hat firmly to his head. This was going to be messy.

"Hey, you know what Clive?" he shouted over the bar. He could hear Clive reloading and pacing back and forth. "I'm going to come out from behind here with my hands up-"

"Paws!" interrupted Clive.

"Sure," sighed Jimmy. "Whatever. You know I'm unarmed, so I'll just come out from behind here, you can put the gun down, we'll have a discussion, man to man- "

"Weasel!"

Jimmy tried to suppress the rage. He always tried, honest to goodness he did. But certain things just really pushed his buttons, and Clive knew that. Later, he would feel bad about what happened next.

The spread on a pellet blaster at five meters is almost exactly forty centimetres between each individual shot. They're manufactured this way. Jimmy ran the numbers, he was good at mental arithmetic. He also factored in the fact that Clive was hammered, only had one eye and could never shoot straight even when he had two.

"Dirty fucking anim-" Clive bellowed, not completing the thought or the sentence before Jimmy jumped from behind the bar, off a framed poster of Wham! and onto the barman's face. Off balance, Clive discharged the gun into his own foot, his toes spreading to the four filthy corners of the bar as he yelped in dismay. Jimmy nimbly landed on the floor.

A girlish shriek devolved into whimpers behind the vintage pinball machine.

"Well, that didn't go well," Jimmy said to himself.

FORTY-FIVE MINUTES EARLIER

Jimmy and Davonne sat in the squad car. Davonne absent-mindedly picked at the mould on the dashboard while Jimmy read the paper.

"We finished our shift ten minutes ago," said Davonne.

"We finish our shift when we've done the job," replied Jimmy without moving his eyes from the tablet.

Davonne sighed deeply as if all the weight of the world was on his shoulders. "I've got gaming night tonight, that's all."

Jimmy grunted. "I'm sure your virgin pals will leave some orcs for you to slay, don't worry."

"It's not orcs, actually," snapped Davonne. "It's Space Commandos and actually it's very cerebral."

"Uh huh. Well, you can all get back to buttfucking each other in VR as soon as we go in here and I have a little conversation with my pal Clive."

"Why? Why do you keep winding this guy up? You know he hates you."

Jimmy waved Davonne off. "He doesn't hate me. We go way back. Did you know when I first arrived in this country, Clive's Dive was the first place I got drunk?"

"Yes," muttered Davonne. "You tell me this every time we come here."

"Do I? Oh. Well, he's a piece of shit but he knows everything that goes on in this town. He's useful, so let's go and ask him about the Dutch shipment then I can go home and you can go to Talos 5, or whatever."

"Thanos 8."

"I don't give a fuck. Get out of the car."

The AQ was a miserable 2.3. So bad that even breath guards weren't touching it. The sensible thing on days like this was to just stay indoors in a cocoon of air conditioning, but some people had to work. Rain sheeted down, as it almost always did, with a greasy shimmer that left you dirtier than it did wet. The two AgOps trotted briskly from the car to the heavy metal doors of the bar, which were locked tight.

"You're going to have to knock, Davonne."

"Why do I always have to knock?"

Jimmy showed Davonne his hands with an irritated look. "Why do you fucking think?"

Davonne nodded and slammed his meaty fist on the talk panel. A weak beep emanated from a dented speaker.

"WHAT."

"Hey man, it's - uh - we're, can we come in?" spluttered Davonne.

"Jesus," spat Jimmy as he hopped up on a barrel next to the door. "Clive! It's Jimmy and the other guy. Let us in we're being boiled alive out here and we both need some synth after a long shift catching bad guys."

Through the crackle of the speaker and the hum of the traffic around them, Jimmy could hear Clive's brain calculate the difference between his hatred of AgOps and his love for credits. The credits won out, and with another anaemic chirp the door released its magnetic lock.

"Bingo!" said Jimmy. "See Davonne? A little bit of charm, a little bit of self-confidence and it's surprising what you can do isn't it?"

Davonne shrugged. Jimmy led the way inside and the door slammed behind them. They were in a neon-lit hallway. Things scurried in dark corners. The smell was definitely piss. The jukebox was playing a Thompson Twins B-Side. Jimmy couldn't sense any other life forms other than Clive in the vicinity.

Jimmy was blessed with a hypersensitive sense of smell. Well, it was more of a curse these days but back in the old country it really helped and it was obvious why evolution had gifted it to him. Right now, it just meant he could enjoy every tangy aspect of the urine floating microscopically through the air.

He wouldn't have needed a particularly educated nose to find Clive. He was at least seventy, with slicked back silver hair and elaborate facial tattoos. The good thing about these tattoos is that they were mood triggered, as most of them were back in the 2030s. If Clive got angry, the serpent that encircled his right eye became red, for example. Jimmy had never seen the serpent any other colour.

They rounded the corner into the main bar area. It was deserted. Clive was resplendent in his kingdom, his string vest stained an impressive number of colours and his leather trousers no doubt as much a part of him as the sweaty hair that liberally covered his scrawny torso.

"Buy a fuckin' drink, then fuck off," barked Clive.

"That's not a nice welcome Clive," chided Jimmy, hopping onto a steel barstool. "We need to talk about your brand."

"Drink."

"I'll have a Mex. What are you having Davonne? Your treat."

"Uh, I'll just have a Kola," stammered Davonne, clearly disgusted and petrified in equal measure.

Clive emptied his nostrils into a drip tray. He slammed two warm metal canisters on the bar top. "Fifty."

"Fifty? What the fuck Clive? Do I get a hand job as well for that?"

"Wouldn't be able to find it you little rat fuck."

"Touché."

Davonne waved his armpiece over the sensor on the bar. An hour's worth of pay disappeared into Clive's drug fund.

"My straw?" enquired Jimmy. "You know I always have

a straw."

"Fucking freak," spat Clive as he turned around and plucked a metal tube from a puddle of brown sticky liquid on the bar behind him. He wiped it feebly with a towel before stabbing it into the top of Jimmy's can.

"Skol!" exclaimed Jimmy before taking a long suck on the straw. The synthohol was warm, acrid and flat. Davonne sipped tentatively at his soft drink, which was also warm, acrid and flat.

"That's the ticket! Now, Clive, while we're here I was wanting to ask you a couple of things."

"I don't work for you no more," snapped Clive.

"Hey man, this isn't work, it's just two old pals catching up," said Jimmy, giving his best impression of a human smile.

"No fuckin' way. Last time we had a little chat, this place got turned over by the Hungarians - I've only just got it fixed up again."

Jimmy nodded sagely, looking around the room. It looked like a tornado had run through a crack den, but he had to give Clive respect for the pride he had in his shitty dive bar. It was far from the worst in town.

"The Dutch brought in a big shipment this week - you heard anything about it?"

"No."

"Nothing?"

"Nothing, you French bastard."

"I'm not French."

"You are a bastard."

Jimmy conceded that point. "You've heard nothing about it? You haven't been approached with a large shipment of something high-profile?"

"No, I haven't. And even if I had been, I wouldn't know what to do with it."

"No, I figured as much - probably a bit out of your league eh Clive?"

Clive visibly bristled. "You don't know fuck all about my

league, you rat. I'm just saying I don't know nothing about a shipment, I don't deal with the Dutch and even if I did, I wouldn't tell you Jack shit because you're a little weasel fuck, you're a freak of nature and you should be drowned in a barrel of your own shit. Now, I've got to go and take a piss, so drink up, go away and don't come back."

Jimmy raised his eyebrows and exhaled slowly as Clive disappeared out of a side door. "I don't think that guy likes me, you know."

"Can we go? I feel myself getting dirtier just standing here," whined Davonne.

"Don't be a pussy," chided Jimmy, then he suddenly sat up on the stool. His nose twitched. They'd only been partners for three months but Davonne had seen this before.

"What is it Jimmy?"

Jimmy's sense of smell hadn't quite been bludgeoned to death by the environs. A new smell had cut across the stale synthohol and vape gas. Flowers. Perfume? Foreign perfume. Or maybe deodorant, something flowery and feminine, and it was coming from beneath them.

Jimmy jumped down from the barstool and got on all fours. His trench coat trailed him through the filth as he followed his nose to the source of the odour. It took him to a large trapdoor just behind the bar.

"Open this," he commanded Davonne, who looked reticent. Davonne hooked one of his fat fingers into the brass ring in the floor and lifted.

Jimmy looked into the darkness of the cellar. Sixty Asian eyes looked back at him through dirt and tears. They heard Clive's hacking cough from the back alleyway. Davonne dropped the trapdoor and they both resumed their original positions just in time for Clive to limp back through the door.

"Be cool," hissed Jimmy to Davonne.

"You still here?" grunted Clive.

"Yeah, you know - I was thinking, about the Dutch

shipment," said Jimmy as nonchalantly as possible.

"What about it?"

"Forget about that. We're just going to enjoy our piss-water and get going."

"Jimmy!" whispered Davonne, "We're not going to ask about the people in the cellar?"

"What the fuck?" said Clive, who's hearing aids were in better shape than they expected. "Who do you think you are, coming into my establishment and throwin' random accusations about?"

"Well," smiled Jimmy. "I'm an Agent Operative of the City, and it's kind of my job to make sure people don't have cellars full of Asian immigrants."

"Oh fuck," gasped Davonne behind him.

Clive roared and reached behind the bar for a pellet blaster. He cocked it and fired just as Davonne dove behind a pinball machine, and Jimmy shot under a nearby table.

"I'm going to kill you, Jimmy!" Clive bellowed. It definitely sounded like he meant it.

"Come quietly Clive, you'd love being back in prison! Free food and sex!" shouted Jimmy from the temporary safety of the bolted down steel table.

"Stop making him angry!" mewled Davonne, illuminated by the fruit machines.

Jimmy saw Clive reloading and took his chance. Diving off the table towards Clive's face, he was dismayed and frustrated to find himself being hit with a swinging rifle. The impact hurt a great deal, and showed Clive still had a good arm even at his advancing years. Jimmy's trajectory was altered, and he slammed into the wall behind the bar, shattering bottles of illegal hooch and trendy smart cocktails.

Clive fired, and stun pellets embedded themselves in the wall and ceiling around Jimmy. The AgOp remembered he was off duty, and therefore not actually being paid for this.

From his vantage point from under the pinball machine,

Davonne could see Clive stalking Jimmy. Clive's stubby Ennol pellet gun was styled after the old-fashioned shotguns, giving him the appearance of Elmer Fudd as he drooled and paced the sticky floor. But he wasn't hunting wabbits, he was hunting Davonne's partner - and Davonne didn't feel particularly well equipped to help.

A lifetime of intense training at City headquarters and all the best neuro-enhancers the AgOps division could afford would have been useful at this point. Unfortunately, Davonne landed this particular gig partly as a punishment for flunking every single physical test he was thrown into, and partly due to the fact his uncle was Clinton Wassell the Third - the City Chief of Agency Operations.

Davonne didn't know his uncle very well, apart from by reputation. The older Wassell was a fearsome bear of a man, who had single handedly pushed the Sicilians out of the City and kept them out, making under the counter deals with the Hungarians instead - which was seen as an improvement because the Hungarians pushed better quality drugs.

This left Davonne in the peculiar position of both being heavily protected in his AgOp role, and the butt of derision and bitterness from his much more qualified colleagues.

And it only got worse when he was partnered with Jimmy the Weasel.

At first, Davonne thought of it as an honour, Jimmy had freshly arrived from Sweden and had aced his Agency training, the first AgOp of his kind in America. Davonne's DNA had vaulted the obstacles to his career in a way his overweight body never could to get him this exclusive gig - partnering America's first UnSapien agent.

However, from his position kneeling in stale, foul smelling liquid under a pinball table this didn't seem like a privilege. The pinball table shouted staccato blasts from Frankie Goes To Hollywood songs and spastically jerked its flippers as if it was enjoying the ongoing drama.

At the count of three, he thought, he was going to crawl out from beneath it, and in an authoritative and de-escalating manner talk Clive into putting the gun down.

One. Davonne edged closer to the edge of the table. This could be the brave action that finally got him the respect he felt he deserved in the locker room.

Two. He raised to a crouch, Clive still had his back to him and had just blasted the bar with a hail of fizzing chemical darts, which made Davonne jump.

Three. Davonne raised himself to his full height, which was not inconsiderable. Opening his palms to face Clive, just like in training, he just about managed to say "Hey."

Then Jimmy jumped onto Clive's face, and Clive's shoe budget permanently halved. Davonne punched his armpiece frantically, summoning backup.

Jimmy and Davonne waited outside the bar while the SOCOs cleaned up inside. It was late now, Davonne's armpiece was blowing up with messages from his squad asking him where he was. He was going to be late again, and his stats would suffer. Still, this was the job, and he knew Jimmy wouldn't let him go even if he asked. He had never seen Jimmy sleep or rest, he was like a dynamo that seemed to gain energy from chaos. But Davonne did sleep, and he needed to quite badly.

"You shouldn't have called it in, Davonne," said Jimmy in a low voice. He was sat on a squad car's roof, picking lint off his wide brimmed hat as he turned it around in his hands.

"What?" he asked, which seemed like a reasonable question. Clive was stretchered past them, screaming obscenities.

"I hadn't finished questioning the witness," said Jimmy. "He was just about to start getting chatty. Trust me."

"Chatty? While he was screaming in agony?"

Jimmy fixed Davonne with a beady stare. "Look, kid. You've got a lot to learn about this job, and this town."

"But- "

"It doesn't matter. Clive had it coming to him anyway."

"Jimmy, we saved all those people! We did good, right?" asked Davonne, smiling hopefully.

"Yeah," replied Jimmy, replacing his hat, "we're the heroes of the fucking hour."

The rain attempted to puncture their awkward silence.

"Can we go?" asked Davonne.

"Sure," said Jimmy. He was about to hop down from the car roof when he smelled something much more intimidating than Clive's putrid drinking establishment. "Fuck."

"What?" asked Davonne, just as Mother emerged from a squad car on the other side of the street.

"Here we go," said Jimmy dejectedly.

Mother strode purposefully across the street, metal pins striking the asphalt hard. Jimmy's nostrils filled with ozone and hot plastic.

"Jimmy the Weasel," spat Mother. "Here we are again."

"Mother, good to see you!" replied Jimmy in his most ingratiating tone. "What brings you to this particular corner of the toilet?"

"You, as always, Agent," Mother's grill pulsed red and purple. "What in the name of Persing happened in there?" she demanded.

"The perp got frisky ma'am, and I had to defend myself."

"You did."

"I did."

"There were two of you, he was a 72-year-old alcoholic, and you couldn't question the witness without him blowing his own leg off?"

"In my defence, ma'am, I've still not been provided with a suitable de-escalation pipe that fits my hands, and Officer Wassell here is a useless piece of shit."

Mother's display pixels were now almost entirely crimson. The drizzle steamed on her battery pack. "Officer Wassell is the only thing keeping you in this country, so I suggest you treat him with a little more respect, or we'll send you back to the Swedish riverbank you came from where you can go back to eating beetles. Understood?"

"Understood, ma'am," Jimmy doffed his hat to his superior.

"We'll clean up here. You can finish your shift." Mother turned to go, then paused. Her head unit rotated back to them. "Good job finding the human cargo, by the way. That's going on your record and you can expect good points on your accounts shortly. The rightful owners of the cargo will be pleased, not that they know or care who or what you are, so don't get too excited."

"I live to serve," smiled Jimmy.

"Thank you ma'am," muttered Davonne. Mother's optical sensors focussed on him and her display mellowed slightly.

"And you, please try and keep your partner flying straight. Prove to your uncle you can do one thing right, at least."

"Yes, ma'am," said Davonne, his eyes fixed on the greasy street.

Mother stalked back to her squad car and was gone.

"Another day, another dollar," chirped Jimmy. "See you tomorrow, kid."

"See you," said Davonne as he watched Jimmy trot off around the neon washed corner and out of sight.

2

It had been 48 hours since the alien spores had infested Alliance Cruiser Spiros. In the dim steel of the command module, Commander Runcie was formulating a plan. If they were going to get off this ship alive, it was going to take a miracle and a lot of firepower.

Fortunately for Runcie, his brightest and best had so far escaped infection and were stood with him around the central console, each up-lit from the soft white glow of the display. The situation didn't look good. Most power lines had been corrupted or severed completely, and transfer nodes were blinking out of existence as they watched, like faulty Christmas tree lights. It was going to be up to Shelton to get those back up. He looked like a linebacker but had the highest cerebral calibration tests of all of them.

Then there was weaponry. Aside from the stun blasters on their hips, they had limited ammunition for the Ellenbergs and the last of the grenades - maybe two or three apiece. A sturdy fire axe was propped up against the navigation pod. Quartermaster Riley was scanning the ship inventory for the location of further supplies.

Runcie was comforted by the presence of his second in command. Stood to his right, Grux the Tellarian was a proud warrior, fiercely loyal and had a keen analytical mind. Grux would die for his commander, Runcie was just hoping he wouldn't need to today.

"Okay, where are we?" said Runcie.

"We've been in worse spots, Commander," gargled Grux.

"That we have, my friend - but we're going to need a miracle this time."

"Sir, good news - we have a cache of 564 ammo on B deck, behind the infirmary," called Riley.

"B deck is 700 meters through the spores," said Shelton, "our chances of getting to it are low."

"You got a better idea?" snapped Riley, "Without ammo we're going to have to sneak past Gods knows how many of them, and you're not the sneaking type."

"Alright people, stay focussed, Shelton's right - we'd never make it to B deck, and the escape pods are in the opposite direction. I've got a plan."

The crew looked at Runcie expectantly.

"We need a distraction - Grux, hit the fire alarms on B deck and A deck, the sprinklers will set off the CO2 blasters, that should make the spores drop to the floor and we can get past while our breathers last."

The crew looked at each other in silence. Shelton was first to speak.

"That's fucking shit."

"Yeah," interjected Grux in a North American accent. "We can't just run past this shit, what kind of plan is that?"

"I'm Commander!" shouted Runcie, "We do my plan!"

"Not if it's a shit plan we don't," said Riley, "this is why we don't let you be Commander, Davonne. You never want to get into a good firefight!"

"That's not true! What about the last campaign when we defeated the Spiderbots on the Desert Moon?"

"You didn't fight shit!" laughed Grux. "You told us to go get 'em then you logged off because your pizza arrived!"

"Ah fuck you guys," said Runcie. He put his hands to his temples and lifted his head off.

"Come on Davonne, don't be a baby!" chided Shelton from Thalos 8, but Davonne had already set his visor down on the table. He rubbed his eyes. It was far too late, he should have gone to bed after his shift, but he was too keyed up by the evening's events.

"Davonne?" came a voice in his headphones. It was Riley, actually supergamer87, actually Marie Dawson from Kent, England.

"What?" said Davonne with a sigh.

"Look, we're on DM, the others are going to blast their way out of the ship, I'm not going."

"Why not?"

"Ah, it's late. I should go to bed."

"Me too," said Davonne, stifling a yawn.

"Sorry about what I said, by the way - I was in character, and I didn't think it was a terrible plan. The problem is some of the other guys in the squad just want to hack n' slay. I don't mind a bit of stealth every now and then."

"Thanks Super," said Davonne, "I guess maybe I should find a new squad, or a new game. The latest Brian Watson one looks good."

"Yeah, it does, maybe I'll join you."

"That would be cool."

"How was work today?" asked supergamer87.

"Well, it sucked man. I don't know why I'm even there. You know I can't tell you anything specific, but my partner is crazy."

"The weasel?"

"Yeah, the weasel."

"That's wild, where did they find a talking weasel? It's so fucking… weird."

"It's a lot weirder than you can possibly imagine. But he's just like a person, a really bad person."

"Well, I think your job sounds interesting."

"Heh, well, it's not boring I guess."

"Listen, I gotta go. You logging on tomorrow night?"

"Yeah, I reckon so, see if we're off this cruiser."

"Watch out for the spores!" laughed supergamer87. Davonne mocked a gargling scream and logged off to supergamer87's tinny laughter.

At just after 3am, Davonne's left forearm started to vibrate. He blearily prodded at his armpiece to silence the notification and saw Jimmy's face on the screen. This was never good news. The last time Jimmy had called him in the middle of the night it was to help him get his tail out of a street grate over at 3rd and Western. The time before that it was because Jimmy wanted to know how to spell 'migration'. He didn't know if weasels were nocturnal or not, but this one never seemed to sleep.

Davonne punched the 'answer' icon.

"Hey, sexual chocolate - hope I'm not interrupting anything," chirped Jimmy.

"I was sleeping," said Davonne, not hiding his annoyance. "What is it?"

"Ah yeah, sorry about that but something's come up. Get dressed and meet me at the AutoDiner on Park Strip."

"Now?"

"No, next Wednesday. Of course now. Come on." Jimmy hung up and the after image of the armpiece's display screen danced over Davonne's ceiling as he blinked himself awake.

He sighed, wondered briefly how his life would have gone if he'd just been good enough to enter the Korean gaming leagues, even at a journeyman level, like he'd always dreamed. When he started it had all been hand controllers, before headsets became sanctioned, and RSI in both his young wrists slowed him down a millisecond or two, just enough to make him an easy target. His average kill ratios dropped slowly at first, as he experimented with SmartVapes to try to get his edge back, but that didn't last as his physical body couldn't keep up with the needs of the games. No amount of Nootropics could counter the crunching in his carpal tunnels. He gained weight he never since managed to lose, his silhouette burned into the wall of Plato's cave forever.

Davonne rolled out of bed and pulled his regulation AgOp navy trousers and white shirt on, retrieved from a floordrobe as tall as his bed. The act of walking past his computer desk activated Hank, his System2000.

"Hey boss, we gonna play a game?"

"Not right now, Hank."

"You want me to play for you?" chirped Hank, blue icons pulsing on the top of the cube in anticipation.

"No, thanks. I gotta go out."

"BeGreater has a special offer - 30% off everything when you spend just 50 credits on any plugin!"

"Ads off."

"Ads paused for 24 hours."

Davonne plucked his car keys from a hook on the wall and left his apartment in darkness. Hank returned to power saving mode.

The AutoDiner sat by the side of 3rd and Western like a smear of pastel in the continual rain. An updated Edward Hopper painting with no staff, just rotating carousels of transparent plastic boxes. Service staff were reserved for only the good establishments that happily passed the minimum wage onto the entitled patrons willing to pay extra for it. As Davonne parked his car in the lot, he saw Jimmy sat on a table in the window, looking visibly agitated.

Davonne shuffled as quickly as he could through the blue-grey drizzle to the diner, and bustled inside, shaking raindrops off his jacket as he approached Jimmy's table.

"What's up, Jimmy? Man, I was sleeping."

"Sit down. You want something to eat?"

"No."

"Hmmm, I could eat. Let me see what's good." Jimmy looked at Davonne expectantly. Davonne looked at Jimmy. Jimmy waved his paws. Davonne, with a look of realisation, clapped his hands. The carousel rerouted itself towards their table and plastic boxes started parading past them.

"Fucking unsapienist, this system."

"That's not even a word. And it's not the diner's fault you can't clap."

Jimmy grumbled incoherently as he peered into each of

the plastic boxes. One took his eye. "That one, there. Get it."

Davonne snatched the plastic box and put it in front of Jimmy. Jimmy daintily removed the cover with his teeth. It was some kind of grey-blue streaked rectangle, with the consistency of rice. Jimmy started gnawing on it.

"So, what is it? You know if you need a human helper, or even an AssistDroid, you can put a requisition form in at the office. I'm not really… down with being dragged out of bed at 3am to be your butler, man."

Jimmy looked up from the food. A fragment was stuck to his nose. "Cool your fucking jets, kid. Don't flatter yourself. I'm hungry but that's not why I called you. I'm in a bit of trouble, and I need - I would like - your help."

"What kind of trouble?"

"Potentially getting killed horribly kind of trouble."

"Fuck Jimmy, what did you do?"

"Well, it's more like what should I have done instead," said Jimmy, tilting his head and squinting.

"Go on," said Davonne, leaning across the table.

Jimmy sighed. "Tonight. Last night, whatever it was. The human cargo in the cellar."

"Yeah, we found it and freed them all, right? So those people will be safe, they'll be OK?"

"Well, I did - you did fuck all - but that's what we did, yeah. But you see, the problem is, that shipment wasn't supposed to be there."

"I don't get it. Of course those people weren't supposed to be in Clive's cellar."

"No, I mean, I think I know how they got there, and it means someone's in trouble."

Davonne screwed up his face. Then realisation dawned on him. "Jimmy, what the… what are you involved with here?"

"Don't worry, we can sort it."

"We?" spluttered Davonne, leaning closer to Jimmy. "How is this my problem if you're involved in human trafficking?"

Jimmy looked offended. "Human trafficking? Listen I might not think much of humans but selling them like cattle ain't my bag either."

Davonne was confused. "I don't get it."

"Look, all you need to know is that shipment didn't go where it was supposed to go. That's gonna make some people a bit cross. So we need to make it right, and you need to help make it right because you're my partner and that's what partners do for each other. Right?"

Davonne resigned himself to a wacky - and most likely fatal - caper. "Right."

"Good man," grinned Jimmy, chewing his food noisily. "So, we need to go and see a friend of mine."

3

"Datsik!"

The guard banged hard on the cage bars with the butt of his gun.

"Datsik! Wake up, time to work!"

In the corner of the gloom a large mass shifted.

"Come on, get dressed. The boss wants to see you. Make yourself presentable."

The mass grunted in a tone so low the guard felt it more than heard it.

"I am tired."

"You can tell that to the boss, now get dressed." The guard clacked out of the room.

The mass lifted its head slowly and sighed. Datsik's eyes were crusted almost shut and he blinked as he tried to acclimatise himself once again to the single bare bulb and sparse straw floor of the cage he called home.

A pile of clothing had been placed in the corner. Datsik raised his bulk and lumbered over to it. As carefully as he could, he pulled the uniform over his thick fur. It consisted of a pair of dusty black overalls, in a fabric that was tough enough to withstand his claws. It was designed in such a way that walking on all fours was uncomfortable and restricted but walking on his hind legs - the way his master preferred it - was less so.

Once dressed, he trudged over to the cage door and pressed a large green button. A buzzer sounded in another room and in the next few moments two more guards arrived and unlocked the door. Like all the men here, they were dressed in black fatigues and carried high-powered assault rifles. Datsik followed them through harshly lit grey concrete tunnels until they arrived at a double steel door. One of the guards swiped his armpiece on the lock and the door opened hydraulically.

Datsik had made this journey many times before. They emerged into a dark wood hallway, dimly lit by high chandeliers. Datsik's legs ached as he lumbered to the end of the hallway, and through double doors flanked by more guards.

They emerged in a grand library, high walls completely covered in bookcases. It was a room so big it was almost impossible to fully illuminate it, as if any light was sucked viciously from its source. Wheeled ladders and a mezzanine gave access to books of every shape, size and vintage. It smelled of damp and old paper and human sweat. Some of the books had bulletholes in their spines.

Datsik's employer sat at a large desk in the centre of the room. The desk was huge, heavy and leather-topped. Datsik had a long-standing desire to throw his boss face-first through this desk, but that wouldn't happen today. Maybe tomorrow. The man looked up from a holographic screen as Datsik entered.

"Datsik! Thank you for joining me. I trust we didn't interrupt anything?"

"Ivanov," growled Datsik.

Ivanov was a thin, bald man in glasses. He reminded Datsik of a bird he knew back in the village, it had a big beak and a loud cry and was constantly fluttering around trying to learn everything - for what reason, Datsik never knew. That fluttering bird got too close to him one day, so he swiped it out of the air and crushed it under his foot. Everything the bird had learned seeped out of its broken body into the mud.

Datsik walked up to the wooden desk.

"Comrade Datsik," said the man. "You look unhappy."

"Yes, Ivanov," replied the bear, politely. "I am indeed unhappy."

Ivanov made a show of remorse and surprise. "But dear comrade, how can this be? Do we not feed you and give you a warm place to sleep?"

"You do," conceded Datsik.

"And, given that you are a bear - an animal - is there anything else you could possibly require?"

Datsik was silent. Ivanov put down his pencil and stood, walking around the desk with his hands behind his back to stand in front of Datsik. With a motion of his head, he dismissed the guards standing by the door, who took their shiny boots and Ennol S15s with them. The hydraulic door locked loudly.

Eight years ago, Datsik had been found wandering the Dagestan mountain ranges by one of Ivanov's remote mineral scouting groups. Datsik had killed two or three humans by the time he was tranquillised. He would have kept on doing so but he felt sleepy so laid down for a nap, and when he woke up he was locked in the back of a truck. He could hear some of the remaining humans talking in the front cab.

Human language wasn't hard to pick up. It was a lot more straightforward than Bear, which is surprisingly nuanced and utilises a much wider frequency spectrum. By the time the truck had shuddered to a stop at a town in the foothills, Datsik knew enough simple Russian to argue his case for release.

"Let go."

"What is this?" cried one of his captors, "Some kind of trick?" Guns were pointed at Datsik once again.

"Let go. Bear go."

A particularly enterprising soldier was the first to realise the worth Datsik represented. "We must get this back to Ivanov!" he cried, "There will be a great reward!"

And indeed there was. The whole mineral scouting party

were executed to ensure their silence. Datsik learned more Russian, and thanks to Ivanov's infinite library learned Dutch, English and Spanish during the next year of captivity.

"I asked you a question, Datsik," said Ivanov. His natural eye glistened in a way that his mechanical one did not. He smiled. "Surely, you are not ungrateful?"

Datsik breathed. Ivanov stepped a little closer.

"Why do you exist, do you think? Don't you ever wonder? Why are you different from the others? Who made you?"

Datsik shrugged.

"There are rumours," Ivanov said in a half-whisper, looking up at the bear, "that we made you. Not the Russians, but humans. That we made you in a laboratory! What do you think about that? Hey? That would make sense, wouldn't it? That we humans would do what we have always done - bend nature to our will, take what we want from it, improve upon it? Imagine that, little orphan Datsik, no mother or father, just a test tube of chemicals!"

Datsik shifted his weight between his rear paws.

"Or maybe, maybe! The testing we do out there in the mountains - we test the weapons, you know - out there in the scrub and the snow, in the worthless land. We fire the weapons and watch from afar as they land and the radiation and the chemicals work together. It's very interesting, Datsik! Very interesting indeed! Is it possible, do you think, that we made you in this way?"

A faint beeping had started, muffled but persistent. Ivanov became more animated, gesticulating up at the bear, his chest almost pressed against him.

"Surely, no God would make something like you Datsik! Hated by his species, an outcast, and equally hated and feared by humankind! No, were we to create you Datsik it would be for the one purpose you currently serve - do destroy, to do our bidding! To kill, to tear apart our enemies, to be loyal until the end - to be a truly worthy Comrade! Am

I right Datsik? Am I right?"

The beeping had been getting steadily louder and now bounced off the walls. Datsik was breathing heavily. His lips had started to pull back over his long, sharp yellow teeth. Sweat soaked the back of his overalls.

"Ha ha! So you do have feelings, bear! You do respond! But you hear that noise, yes?" crowed Ivanov. "Beep, beep, beep! You hear that as well as I do, and you know what it means."

Datsik reached a paw to the back of his neck. Once again he thought about tearing the tiny nuclear device from the base of his skull, or just rending Ivanov limb from limb anyway. But self-preservation stopped him. Self-preservation and curiosity, for he was a curious bear.

"I would advise you to calm down, my friend. I would hate to see your wonderful head pop off your body. Remember I brought you here to protect me at all costs, that little beep reminds you of that. I for one feel very good about this! To know that if ever I am in danger, you are in so much more. I think it creates a real bond between us, don't you?"

"In a way," mumbled Datsik.

Ivanov laughed and patted Datsik's massive chest. "In a way, yes. You are a freak of science, or maybe of nature, but I can't deny you are very useful indeed. Long may our arrangement continue."

Ivanov took his seat back behind his wooden desk and exhaled noisily. The beeping was starting to subside.

"What do you want?" asked the bear.

"To business then! We have a new job to do, you and I. We have a problem."

"Problem?" rumbled Datsik.

"Yes. Someone is interfering with our shipments. This is not acceptable."

"Okay."

"Would you like to help, Datsik?"

"No."

Ivanov smiled thinly. "I was really asking only out of politeness. You know you must do what I say."

"Yes."

"Good. The men will prepare you for the trip. We leave tomorrow."

Datsik turned and plodded towards the door. Ivanov stood and called to him. "It will be fun, comrade!"

Datsik grunted, and thought again of the fluttering bird.

4

Bravilor Bonamat tripped over a pile of pizza boxes on the way to his frame. His apartment, in one of the worst areas of Little London, which was in one of the worst areas of the City, would have been tiny even without the wall full of salvaged tech or the floor full of garbage.

A beige VDU was blinking a notification - a pickup from Johnny's was ready. He smiled and jabbed at his armpiece to summon an InstaCab. Johnny always kept the best shit for him, usually stuff he didn't understand or was frightened of, which was just the kind of thing Bravilor could use. He grabbed his leather jacket from a hook by the door. The nearby refrigerator sensed his location and seductively advertised a discount on noodles.

By the time he'd jumped down the last few concrete steps to the front door, the InstaCab was outside, humming erratically. It was covered in gang signs and graffiti and had detritus artfully piled on top of it. He got in. By his reckoning he had time to get to Johnny's, pick up the merchandise and still get to the club in time for his shift. The InstaCab whirred and juddered through the backstreets. Dense Polish muzak dripped from the steel speaker grills in the doors. Through the haze and drizzle running down the plexiglass, Bravilor watched drug deals go down, street vendors peddling fake implants and AgOps running down perps. He loved this City.

The car staggered to a halt. "You have been charged 832

credits for this journey. Thank you for using InstaCab! Also, brushing your teeth doesn't have to be a chore with- "

Bravilor absentmindedly checked his arm - the credit blocker was still working perfectly. No charge today. Pulling his jacket over his head he dashed from the cab to Johnny's Antique Shop.

The shop did indeed deal in antiques, despite the fact it looked like any pawn shop in any city at any time. Random items covered every flat surface and every wall. Objects dangled from the ceiling. Everything had a price card, that scrolled and flashed the latest price, determined by simple algorithms that searched the net for every other price now and historically. It was impossible to get a better deal - mainly because these price cards fed purchase data back to the net, and demand was monitored. Just looking at an item too long in any shop in the world would boost its sale price for everyone by a few credits. It was a clever system, but like any system, could be hacked.

In this case, the hack was a simple Social Engineering one. Johnny sold items to Bravilor in exchange for favours, not credits. In a return to the old feudal bartering system that thumbed its nose at both the City and world governments in equal measure, most street trade was done this way. It had brought the high street back from the dead some fifty years after it had died, and given people like Johnny a source of income, after a fashion.

"Johnny!" called Bravilor as he shut the door behind him and shook grey rain from his back. From around a corner wheeled the proprietor. His eyes were red slits and his long lank hair sat in his lap as he navigated the small shop in his manual wheelchair. Johnny had no legs from the knees down, but nobody Brav knew had ever asked why - nor had Johnny offered the information. He looked too young to be a veteran of any of the recent wars, so Johnny assumed some kind of necrosis from bad gas vapes.

"Bravilor Bonamat, my man!" said Johnny, giving Bravilor an elaborate handshake. "I've got something interesting for you my friend."

Johnny returned to behind the counter and waited a few seconds for the lifting platform to bring him up to the correct height. He pulled something out from under the counter and laid it on the scarred desktop. "What do you think?"

"Some kind of frame card, looks industrial? Where did you get it?"

"Ha ha come on man, you know I can't tell you that!"

"Yeah, sure, stupid of me to ask." Bravilor turned the plastic card over in his fingers. It was gunmetal grey, and there was Japanese printed on the back. He'd never seen anything like it before, and he'd seen just about every piece of tech from the last 50 years. "I reckon I've got an adaptor that will read this."

"You want it?" asked Johnny.

"Maybe. How much?"

"The usual," grinned Johnny, showing his missing teeth.

"Shit, that's expensive," joked Bravilor. He thought about it, flicked his blue-black fringe out of his eyes. "Okay man, I'll take it. But if it fries my frame I'll hold you responsible."

"No fuckin' refunds, man," chuckled Johnny.

"Yeah, yeah, SOP. Right, I'd better get to work or I'm fucked."

"Sadia on tonight?" asked Johnny.

"Yeah, you coming down?"

"Nah man, I'm higher than giraffe pussy right now, I can't make it outside."

Bravilor laughed. "Sure thing my brother, you do you. Okay I'm gonna blast. Keep me posted if you get anything else in." He slipped the card into his jacket pocket and zipped it closed.

The club was a short walk away, so Bravilor thought he'd brave the rain and get there on foot. He knew this part of Little London like the back of his hand, and most of the people in it, so it was low risk. A few blocks later he saw Rancids loom in the distance.

Rancids wasn't owned by someone called Rancid. Rather it was named after its clientele. Even by Little London standards this place was a cess pit. Through the buffeting sheets of toxic drizzle, Bravilor could see the flickering sign, in cold blue, reflecting off the wet leather of the people waiting in line outside.

Fluffy wasn't pleased to see him, but then he never was.

"You're fuckin' late again Brav you little punk," was how the bouncer greeted him. He was a brick wall of a man, with no discernible neck.

"No I'm not, Fluff. I start at half past on Saturdays."

"It's 32 minutes past, check that piece of shit armpiece."

Bravilor checked, and Fluffy was indeed correct. But Fluffy had one of the first HUD implants, one of the few that hadn't caused retinal cancer yet, so he always knew what time it was.

"Well, can't stop and chat Fluff, better get to work," grinned Bravilor, patting Fluffy's massive bicep as he slipped past the bouncer and the start of the line to enter the club.

Standing in the scanning booth, waiting for the blue light to wash over him, Bravilor thought about the card in his pocket. He was hoping it was easily flippable because he could use the credits. Rent was due and not paying it wasn't an option as the electronic locks on his apartment would simply stop working as soon as the funds ran dry. The booth told him not only was he not armed, but 87% of surface-dwelling parasites had now been eradicated. He loped through the hissing slide door into the gloom.

There were already some clientele here, and they were strapping themselves eagerly to the large black frequency pods. A few dozen others were at the bar, swiping their armpieces and inhaling psychotropic chemical cocktails from gas booths embedded in the bar top. Everyone was gearing up for a fun night of being vibrated by sub-sonic music until they either passed out, or it was closing time.

Bravilor made his way through the room, his boots sounding loud in the relative silence. He could see Heatrae Sadia in the DJ booth, her angular 6 foot 2 frame hunched over her control panels like a mother spider. As he got closer he noted she looked in a bad mood. But Sadia was always in a bad mood.

"Hey, Sadia - how's it going?" said Bravilor, peering over the edge of her platform.

"Fuck off, Brav. I'm busy," deadpanned Sadia in her Eastern European drawl. "And you're late."

"But- "

"Three minutes. And Sporry wants to see you."

"Fuck."

"Yes," said Sadia with a smirk as her thin white hands moved over the controls. "You probably are, now go away."

"You coming down the pits later?" asked Bravilor as casually as he could.

"Maybe," replied Sadia.

"Cool, see you then," said Bravilor as he jumped down off the platform and looked up to the office where his boss was waiting for him. It was situated on the first floor, surrounded by a gantry, from which the owner of the club could survey his kingdom. Bravilor couldn't see anything through the one-way windows. He trudged up the steel steps and came to the office door, bulletproof and scarred to show its usefulness. He knocked.

The door was opened by Chino, Mr Sporry's bodyguard, right hand man and lover. Chino beckoned Bravilor in with his pistol. Bravilor didn't like guns, but this wasn't unusual behaviour for Chino, who almost permanently held a weapon for reasons that became more obvious the more you learned about his employer's activity.

Hugo Sporry was sat on the edge of his desk, looking out of the window into the club below. He was eating a burrito and addressed Bravilor around mouthfuls.

"Bravilor Bonamat!" he exclaimed. "How are you?"

"I'm… I'm good thanks Mr Sporry, you wanted to see me?"

"I did. I did. How's the line looking?"

"Looking good, couple of hundred at least."

"That is good. You got anything special planned for tonight?" asked Sporry, turning to Bravilor. Bravilor did not.

"Yes! Been working on some new algorithms, there's a few new spectrum combinations I want to try out."

"Sounds great, sounds great kid. You know I don't understand any of that shit, but if our customers enjoy it, then that's what I'm interested in." Sporry smiled widely at Bravilor with his cheeks full of food. He looked like a round, balding hamster. "Anyway, that's not why I asked you to come see me. I need another little favour."

Bravilor's heart dropped to his stomach. This was what he was afraid of. Being a good computer hacker and hardware engineer was as much of a curse as a blessing in his experience. He only really got into building frames as a hobby, like most of the Pit Kids. You find what you can use in the City junk pits, you repurpose it for fun or sometimes for credits. But this was worse.

"You did pretty good for me in the past kid, and I know how you youngsters love to trade in favours not credits, and that suits me good too - because I don't want to give you any credits." Sporry finished the burrito and rolled the wrapper up into a tight ball with his thick stubby fingers. He threw the ball of foil at Chino, who batted it away with his gun and looked annoyed.

"You know the last favour you did for me?" asked Sporry, waddling back behind an elaborate faux-leather-topped desk and pulling a tablet out of a drawer. "Didn't go so good."

Bravilor swallowed hard.

"Hey, nothing to do with you kid," reassured Sporry. "You did everything real perfect. Nah, some external forces got involved, shall we say. My customers are pretty pissed. But these things happen in business. I just need to get another shipment of goods is all."

Bravilor cleared his throat. "So, you want me to do the same again?"

Sporry waved a ring-encrusted finger at him. "You are a smart kid! Not just a lightshow guy! Yes, young Bonamat, you will get into the shipping service frame and reroute another container for me, to my private docks, and for this I will grant you another favour. What a deal!"

"So then I'll have two favours?"

"Fuck no kid, you trying to roll me over? You didn't use the last one, that's on you. Make sure you call up this new favour before you lose it. That's a valuable life lesson for you there, son."

They both knew that there was no way Bravilor would ever ask Sporry for anything, and no way Sporry would do anything for Bravilor if he did. But this was the balance of power.

"Sure, Mr Sporry. I can do that. Sounds like… sounds like a good deal."

"You bet your ass it is, Bravilor. As soon as I get the details of the next shipment, I'll let you know. No fuckups kid, and no talking to nobody about our little arrangement, OK?"

"Understood, Mr Sporry."

"Now, Chino - get this kid a blast," said Sporry, motioning for Chino to pass one of the wall-mounted breathers across.

"Uh, no thank you," said Bravilor as politely as he could. "I don't, I mean not before a shift."

Chino looked both disgusted and amused. "Faggot."

"Hey, no - that's true professionalism Chino, you could learn that from this boy!" Chino's dark eyes narrowed at Bravilor. Another enemy he didn't need. Tonight was going great.

"I better get to my decks Mr Sporry," said Bravilor.

"Yes! Yes, go boy. Go do your… thing," effused Sporry, waving his hands vaguely in the air. Bravilor shut the thick metal door behind him and finally breathed. His body felt heavier, somehow.

The rest of his shift was a blur. He did find some new algorithms and they worked out well. He downloaded the code from his armpiece to the Richter 8100 light generators and the control desk synced them with the oscillators Sadia was controlling on the other side of the dance floor. Subtle changes in waveforms pulsed through the ten obelisks, decorated like gothic Christmas trees with the ragged bodies of the drug-soaked clientele. Bravilor's lightshow pulsed and streamed colours and tones across the floors and ceilings. The customers who were still conscious lolled their heads and drooled in appreciation. It was a good crowd tonight.

Bravilor felt uneasy about his latest assignment from Mr Sporry. He'd worked at Rancids for four years, and Sporry had owned it for three after a bloody gun battle with the previous crime family. The new boss quickly determined Bravilor's usefulness was twofold - he could run the lighting decks and he could make pretty much any technology talk to any other technology from the past fifty or so years.

At first the requests were benign enough. Remove bugs from the club's frame, reset the service codes on the breather pumps when they got full of saliva and so on. Then a layer of secrecy was introduced. Access this IP address, download this data but don't decrypt it. That kind of thing. To date, Bravilor had not received anything in return, apart from keeping his job and his life.

Across the room, Heatrae Sadia was wrapping up her set into a climax of pulsing folded sine waves. The straps on the frequency pods creaked, the people attached to them moaned, then the air became still as the pods were switched off. You never noticed when you came into the room, but the air molecules were always moving in regimented patterns. Now they had gone back to their glorious randomness and it felt more natural to breathe again. The smells of the bar crept back up Bravilor's nostrils -

chemicals, sweat, cum.

Fluffy was unstrapping the customers and slapping them to wake them up, or in some cases dragging them out to the street by their ankles, as Bravilor approached Sadia. She was packing her headphones into her bag and winding up cable.

"Great set, Sadia," he said, moving his fringe out of his eyes and smiling. Sadia didn't look up.

"Thanks. Lights were good too."

Bravilor grinned. "Really? Cool, I had some new code in there tonight-" he started, but Sadia was already walking away. He resisted the urge to follow her and appear desperate. Instead, he just watched her angular frame stalk out of the back door. She moved like she was made of too few polygons. He sighed. It was 2am and he still had work to do.

5

Davonne and Jimmy were in the car, travelling across town. The rain had stopped, but the plexiglass windows were dripping condensation into the footwells. Everything was perpetually damp and sour, but this was City life. Davonne drove, Jimmy sat on top of a box strapped into the passenger seat so he could see out of the windows. The car was mostly silent.

"So," said Davonne, "who are we going to see?"

"Friend of mine, very clever character. He's going to help us put this right. Or, wrong. Whatever."

"How?"

"You'll see."

"Will there be more violence?" asked Davonne, deadpan.

"I cannot guarantee that there won't be," said Jimmy.

"Jimmy, we're trained to de-escalate."

"*You're* trained to de-escalate, Davonne. That's your thing. I'm a fucking weasel, I'm only small, and you nasty humans are so big and scary." Jimmy mocked.

"Thank Persing you're too small to hold a gun," snapped Davonne.

"Whatever," sighed Jimmy.

A long moment passed. They watched the rooftops slide silently beneath them as they cruised over the City. The haze on the horizon, illuminated by the countless artificial lights of human presence gave the vista an undeserved halo.

Davonne glanced at Jimmy. "Say, what's it like?"

"What's what like?" replied Jimmy, not shifting his gaze from the scrolling scenery.

"You know, being you. Here. Do you like it? Do you ever wish you were back where you came from?"

Jimmy sighed and removed his hat. He scratched at the fur on his head. "I don't know, Davonne. I guess it's fine. Yeah, it's fine."

They dropped into silence again. Another AgOp cruiser slid beneath them, large numbers on the roof identifying it as Vice division, heading towards the red light districts of Little London.

"You know what?" continued Jimmy, "It's not actually fucking fine. Let me tell you something about me you might not know, Davonne. I've never been able to speak my own language. Yeah, that's right, as soon as I was old enough I realised that I couldn't understand a fucking thing my parents or my brothers and sisters said to me. They just fucking squeaked and I had no idea what they were talking about. And they were stupid, Davonne. So fucking stupid. Just scurrying around all day eating bugs and all that shit. I was there, thinking 'there has to be more to life than this'."

Davonne stared, wide-eyed at Jimmy. "Holy shit."

"Yeah, exactly. And I noticed that none of the other weasels had one of these-" he pointed to the transponder unit on his right leg. "I always remembered having it, and it didn't seem strange that nobody else did. Anyway, after a while, obviously I was rejected. I wasn't picking up on the group's routines. I was a bad weasel, basically. Didn't fit the mould, you see. So that was that. Kicked out. Bad weasel."

"Man," said Davonne shaking his head. He didn't know what else to say.

"But you know what's funny? The very same day I was chased out of the area by sharp teeth and claws, and the angry hissing of my own fucking mother, I was scooped up into a white plastic cage by some scientist dudes, drugged and woke up here. Funny story, huh?"

"Who were they?" asked Davonne.

"Fuck knows. But ever since then, I'm like - what the fuck am I?"

"Yeah, like are you a human trapped in a weasel's body, or something?"

"Don't be fucking ridiculous Davonne," admonished Jimmy, knitting his brow. "How would that even work."

"Do you want to find out?" asked Davonne, afraid of the answer.

Jimmy sniffed and looked out of the window again. "Nah. It wouldn't help me. I've got a lifespan of about 12 years, Davonne. I could spend all of them looking for answers and I'd be no better off than I am now. I'm lucky, really. I've got a job, I've got food and shelter. I'm doing OK."

"Well, I guess- "

"The thing is," Jimmy continued, "it's not just that I can understand and speak human language, I think like you guys. I don't think like a weasel - you get me? It's like… you and I run the same operating system on different hardware, you see?"

Davonne nodded.

"And for some reason, maybe because of that, I feel trapped in this body. It pisses me off that I don't have things like opposable thumbs - those things seem fucking useful, Davonne. So somehow I'm here, in this fucking disgusting metal and plastic City, with the body of a wild animal, being asked to do human things. It's fucked."

"I still don't understand how you ended up an Agent," said Davonne, then caught himself. "I mean, you're real good at it, but it seems a strange choice."

Jimmy laughed. He didn't laugh often but it always caught Davonne off-guard. It was high and chattering. "There's no choice, partner. No choice at all. That's the story of my fucking life. I didn't choose to be different, I didn't choose to be kicked out of my family and I didn't choose to be a fucking AgOp, interacting with the very worst examples of human existence. I have literally no idea who decided I should do it, but I woke up in that white plastic cage and I was in City HQ and the training just started, so I went along with it because I was young and scared and had no other options."

"Then," Jimmy spat, "I learned about bills, and rent, and finding a home - you can't just rock up at the riverbank and collect a bunch of moss and twigs, right? And yeah, I guess the Agency helped a bit with that and they got me set up but that was it. And that's been me ever since. I go home, I come into work, I try not to get shot. The end."

Davonne was taken aback by Jimmy's candour. This was probably the longest conversation they'd ever had. He felt like he should share in return.

"Well, I guess I sympathise about the family rejection thing. My uncle- "

"Yeah yeah," interrupted Jimmy. "He's SuperCop, I know. The other boys at HQ filled me in on that."

"Yeah," continued Davonne. "I wouldn't have this job if it wasn't for him, I know that. But he never returns my calls, if there are family events I don't get to hear about them. I scraped through basic training, he got me this job at the bottom of the ladder and I guess I'll stay here."

Jimmy inhaled through his sharp front teeth. "You're a smart guy, Davonne, but you're fucking lazy. That's your problem. You need to shift that weight, my man. Get fit, get lean, like me. This is a physical job we're doing, you get me?"

"Thanks for the tough love, Jimmy," said Davonne, trying to hide the hurt from his voice.

Jimmy chattered again. "Chill out my man, you do good. I mean, you could have been a bit more proactive with the whole Clive situation, but I've already forgiven you for that. Stick with me, kid, I'll see you right."

"So, are there more of you?" asked Davonne.

"More weasels?"

"No, well yeah. More talking animals."

"I've heard there might be a dog somewhere, and maybe a bear. Other than that, I don't know. It's not like we have a Intrachat group or anything."

"So weird," said Davonne, shaking his head.

"It's a weird world, my man," said Jimmy.

Bravilor Bonamat kicked the door of his apartment shut behind him and put the pizza box on the table, on top of all the others. He kicked off his boots and dropped into his computer chair. Chewing on a pizza crust, he stabbed at the beige mechanical keyboard of his frame with fingerless gloved hands.

Bravilor's frame was much like any other Pit Kid's. A wall of mismatched computer hardware from previous decades, jury-rigged together in fun and interesting ways, designed to manipulate the new reality through the medium of bits and bytes. The true fundamental building blocks of the world. Quantum theory, even string theory had largely been abandoned in favour of digital theory the previous decade. Leading scientists determined that as the human brain ran off tiny electrical impulses, these were analogous to the computers we had built for ourselves in the 21st century, not through some kind of accident but because we were imitating ourselves. We were creating tools in our own image, like the Gods did in the pre-secular world.

In this new world, the act of creation had become democratised as anyone with access to hardware and the requisite skill could create communication channels between humans, create spaces in which they interacted, control currency and trade, manipulate politics and opinion, and ultimately how the human world worked and ran.

Bravilor wasn't interested in creating the world, but he was interested in fucking it up. Since he was a kid he'd resented authority. Multiple foster homes - which represented a battle to survive, to scrape and scratch himself to the top of a barrel of unwanted children - left him with a cold distaste for human connection. There were exceptions of course, like Sadia or Johnny. But he was grown up now, 22 years old by his best guess, and he decided long ago he wasn't the kid getting beaten by yet another foster dad in the back room of some condo up and down the West coast.

His frame, then, was his physical presence in the world. Not just a room with a view but a tool and a weapon with which to influence his surroundings. It was useless without knowledge and skill, of course, and he had Brett Oka to thank for that. Brett was another kid, a couple of years older, that he had shared a motel with during a year stop off between temporary parents. A genius by any measure, Brett had sat down with Bravilor night after night and showed him the beauty of computing, the raw, basic flow of electrons through switches and logic gates that blown up and writ large made anything possible. Ten years ago, Brett had told Bravilor that the future would live in databases. He was right before he even said it.

Dim LED lights spotted the racks of equipment and blinked to each other. Bravilor leant across and lifted a thick ribbon cable to read a numeric display. He remembered the card in his jacket pocket, secured the last pizza crust between his teeth and fished it out. He rubbed the contacts on his black jeans to clean them and pushed it into one of the card reader slots in the frame's I/O module.

The VDU blinked, flashed and showed a command prompt. Bravilor typed in the relevant commands to verify the integrity of the card. To his surprise it came back as functional and clean. This was rare, especially with merchandise he got from Johnny.

He hit the key combination for LOAD.

At first nothing happened. Bravilor squinted at the read/write access indicators on the machine, they flickered with activity. Maybe the VDU had given up. He slapped the side of the plastic case. The image jumped and resolved itself. Bravilor chuckled as the image rolled and finally stabilised.

On the screen was a green on black wireframe model of a turtle. It was very low resolution, pretty retro/vintage style, which Bravilor appreciated. The turtle model slowly rotated. The simple green on black geometrics described the beak, the weak chin, the shell, the flippers impotently waving gently in the negative space.

Bravilor watched the wireframe rotate. Pretty weird, obviously not military/industrial as he was expecting. He punched the usual common key combinations. Nothing. He leant to his right to scrutinise another display screen. Sensors were all quiet. Was this really it? Whatever favour Johnny would expect in payment, this was looking like a bad deal.

Out of habit Bravilor pushed back the sleeve of his jacket to run a net search on his armpiece. He stalled at the query. Sighing, he spotted the time. It was 4am again. It was always 4am it seemed. No time. He should sleep.

He moved a collection of random items off his decaying couch, including his headset. No gaming for him tonight, besides last night on Thalos 8 his Commander flipped out and went AWOL and he couldn't be bothered with any more drama right now. He removed his leather jacket and threw it over the chair, then curled up to sleep with the wireframe rotating slowly on the VDU screen, its reassuring green glow bathing the room.

Bravilor Bonamat had crazy dreams. He never usually dreamed at all, but this night was different.

The dream he remembered most clearly consisted of a boat ride through some enormous caverns. The roof was ridged and bright red. In the boat were Brett Oka and the wireframe turtle, who was still a wireframe but somehow had mass, and could physically sit in the small wooden boat with Brett and himself. Brett and the turtle sat opposite Bravilor as he was rowing the boat deeper and deeper into the red caves. Brett was dressed in his usual beige sweater over a checked shirt, his grey trousers tight over his chubby thighs.

"You see, Brav," Brett was saying. "There were always three spheres of existence. The geosphere, which is the

Earth, or whatever planet you happened to live on. This was the rock and the soil and the seas, where things lived. The geosphere changes very slowly, but it does change - cliffs erode from the tides, tectonic plates shift and create land masses, that kind of thing."

Brett adjusted his glasses. "The next sphere above that is the biosphere - this is all the living things that exist in the geosphere, and they rely on the environment there to survive, for shelter and resources. The biosphere can also influence the geosphere by mining, farming, poisoning it with chemicals they have created, and so on. The geosphere, in turn, can affect the biosphere - think natural disasters, or the movement of species across it to find favourable areas for living."

The wireframe turtle sat impassively, it seemed it was listening to Brett with a vague, Mona Lisa smile. It occasionally flickered, as if to remind Brav it was no more or less real than Brett at this point. Even in the dream Brav missed Brett. He kept rowing. The oars disappeared into the black water on every pull. The water was thick.

"The third sphere, Brav, is the noosphere. This is the sphere of human thought. The noosphere affects the biosphere as we create medicines to make ourselves live longer, or drugs to kill ourselves, or invent new hunting mechanisms to kill other species. The noosphere can similarly affect the geosphere - we create maps and road networks to control it. But, of course, the geosphere can influence the noosphere, for example, sacred stone circles and the biosphere affects the noosphere as we develop bigger and better brains as we evolve. Are you getting all this?"

Brav nodded, but in the dream he couldn't think of anything to say. The walls and ceiling were getting closer he thought. The walls were also red, and wet.

Brett leaned in closer, conspiratorially. "But there's a new sphere now, Brav. And it's the most influential of all. It's the datasphere. The collected data about everything, from everything. It's not just the ability to assess it or utilise it in the noosphere, it's the data itself. We've spent our entire lifetime as a species collecting it, from the first cave painting really - and within the past few centuries this has accelerated to incomprehensible levels. Now, the weight of this collected data has become…" Brett became uncharacteristically lost for words, and gesticulated until something suitable came to him, "significant."

Brav raised his dream eyebrows and shrugged. Looking at the wireframe turtle, he could have sworn it smiled a little more at this. Brett looked annoyed, like he did when Brav couldn't understand a programming concept.

"Don't you get it, Brav?" asked Brett, smiling. "Data. There's so much of it, and now, thanks to the net, it all knows about itself. Ever since we connected two computers together, no - ever since the Guttenberg press, we've been stacking books next to each other, storing bits and bytes on magnetic tape, uploading to the cloud. The data can see itself, and with enough of it, it was inevitable that this would happen."

Bravilor desperately wanted to ask, 'What would happen?' but his jaw wouldn't open. It seemed that Brett heard him anyway. Brett smiled and looked at the wireframe for the first time. He smiled at the turtle.

"This," he said. "Oh look, we're here."

Bravilor looked past him. The cave was now very small, the water seemed thicker and darker than it should be. In the dim light up ahead, he saw what looked to be some kind of sand bank, their destination.

The boat gently grounded itself on the land and Brett got out, then the wireframe flopped onto the bank. Brav stepped off the boat and to his surprise the ground was soft and moist. Looking back, he saw the sides of the boat were red with what looked like blood.

"Come on, time to get back," said Brett cheerily.

The wireframe turtle stood on its hind legs and held out its flipper to Bravilor. He didn't know what to do. He looked at Brett. Brett nodded reassuringly. Bravilor leant down, reached out his hand and grasped the turtle's flipper. To his surprise, it was warm. The jagged vectors that comprised it were hard edged and there was no substance between them. But despite this, it made him feel good. Safe. The turtle's black eyes looked at him, and there was a depth to them.

Brett motioned for them to walk into the darkness ahead, and he led the way. Bravilor and the wireframe turtle followed him, slowly.

Bravilor had so many questions, but before he could answer, a huge gaping slash started to open ahead of them and light was pouring in. As the warm yellow light started to illuminate the chamber, Brav could see the top and bottom edges of the opening were lined with sharp white teeth.

Then he woke up. He blearily checked his armpiece. 8am, and the notification from Sporry still blinked obnoxiously in the top right corner as if to remind him it wasn't going away. He looked across the room. The wireframe was still slowly spinning as it had been before.

He should do some work.

6

Julie Yang huddled in the darkness. The smell of human sweat, waste and fear filled her nostrils, as it had for the past three days. At least she was warm now - the previous two nights sat in a container at the docks were ferociously cold. Around her, small voices spoke in languages she didn't understand, but their terror surpassed any language barrier.

Incredibly, this wasn't the worst undercover operation she'd been assigned to. Four years ago she was asked to pose as a sex worker at one of the knocking shops in Little London, and while she managed to avoid any sexual activity herself, she had to administer gas enemas to scores of decaying mottled businessmen with all the associated unpleasantness you might imagine. At least sat in this cellar she wasn't dressed in a bunny outfit feeding tubes up middle-aged asses.

Despite the occasional challenging assignment, Julie enjoyed her job at the Agency. She wasn't technically an Operative, working as she did in the Research and Information Gathering department, but she was damn close to it and aspired to wear the barcode one day. Her parents instilled in her a strong work ethic and a reluctance to complain, regardless of how uncomfortable or unpleasant her circumstances might get.

In the container, small white shafts of light would stab through the dusty air during the daytime. This was just enough light to make out that there were perhaps 30 people in the metal crate. All of Asian origin, a variety of ages and genders. They all wore armpieces, but every one of them was black, inert, disconnected. Julie's own armpiece was also a dead steel and plastic weight. She had no way of contacting the office, or recording any of the information she gathered, but knew she could rely on her RIG memory and retention training.

The preparation for this assignment had gone very smoothly. The Agency wanted to get to the source of a rise in human trafficking, and Julie was selected as a kind of human tracking device. Three nights ago she was brought in under cover of darkness and camera blockers and dropped into the container through a hatch on the roof. This prompted a large outcry from the terrified inhabitants, not least because she involuntarily landed on a few of them. Once the hatch was slammed shut again and locked, she had crawled to a small patch of free space and sat hugging her knees for warmth, and waited.

One thing she did regret - and it was a small thing - was wearing deodorant. As soon as she dropped in, the stench of the others had hit her like a soggy blanket. Hopefully her own floral scent would be subsumed into this miasma before the container was eventually opened.

Yesterday the container moved. She felt herself being hoisted high into the air, people crying out in dismay and terror, and placed with a resounding clang onto a platform, which moved under the whine of heavy electric motors. After precisely 5 hours, 23 minutes, and travelling broadly North-West, the transporter came to a halt. To further shrieks and incomprehensible cries, the end of the container was swung open in an explosion of white light. By the time everyone's eyes had adjusted to the daylight they had been ushered down an alley by Hispanic men with shiny chrome guns, down through a trapdoor and were back in darkness once again.

At least this darkness was warm. By Julie's reckoning - and she was paid to be good at exactly this - she was now beneath Clive's Dive in Little London. The GPS sensors embedded in her scalp confirmed this silently to her handlers back at the office.

She didn't want to be unkind but she wished the other inhabitants of the cellar would be quiet so she could gather audio data. Her assignment had turned from a location determination to perpetrator identification mode at this point, just as the handbooks dictated. First figure out where you are, then figure out who is involved.

A long day passed. She urinated in the corner. Hunger gnawed at her stomach, but the slow-release micronutrients she had swallowed before leaving HQ would prevent any danger of malnutrition. Dehydration was more of a risk, so she was carefully rationing the water pouches installed under the skin of her forearms, and sucking at them as inconspicuously as she could in the near pitch black.

Early the following morning, Julie heard voices from beyond the hatch.

Ivanov was doing a word search on his armpiece in the back of the car. Datsik's huge bulk was sat on the floor opposite, where some seats used to be. Datsik looked uncomfortable, and indeed he was, almost all the time. The human environment seemed constantly cramped, hot, and irritating in a variety of ways. He never missed home, however, as that was worse. He tried not to think about the mountains, or what used to be his family. It was best just to think about the matters at hand. Datsik was a Stoic bear.

When he was first captured by the Russians and brought to the City, random books were pushed through his cage bars at an alarming rate, and Datsik read them all. From his captors' point of view, they were upgrading their new weapon. From his point of view, he was learning about the new world he found himself in.

Datsik was a good, fast reader. He would lay each paper book in turn on the floor of his cage and pin the pages open with two massive black claws. He would read as long as there was sufficient light to do so, or as long as the damp paper would hold together. Some books were in other languages, so he taught himself what he needed to comprehend those too. Datsik became quite expert in French cooking, the novels of Barbara Cartland, how to repair a Honda C50 motorbike, the best way to prepare for pregnancy and many other things. But his favourite books were those on human philosophy. He considered these a window into the inner workings of the human mind, which from his perspective could be highly valuable if this was to be his new life.

Philosophically, Datsik had a lot in common with the ancient stories he had read about another bear, who was friends with a baby pig. Their stories inspired him to take life as it came and to accept existence as it was, rather than how he wanted it to be. There was also a tiger and a donkey but they didn't interest him as much. He tried to relate the adventures of the bear in the book with his own. It was a stretch, as Pooh didn't rip many people's throats out, but aside from that, there were some parallels.

Datsik's 100 Acre Wood was a 20 foot by 20 foot concrete floored cage. His Piglet were a few cockroaches and his Owl was a scruffy looking bird that would occasionally alight on the high window ledge. None of the other creatures engaged him in conversation, so it was more of an academic exercise.

Now, he was with Christopher Robin in the back of a black car, the motor noise irritating his ears, as they cruised along on their way to visit someone or other. Maybe this time it would be a nice meeting, maybe there would be honey - he had never tasted honey, but it sounded amazing - and maybe he would have an adventure.

Datsik cleared his throat. Ivanov didn't look up from his puzzle. He was dressed in a slim grey suit with a white polo neck underneath, still looking like a wise bird. It wasn't how Christopher Robin was described in the books, but it was close enough.

"Where are we going?" rumbled the bear.

"We are going to see someone who might have some information for us, comrade Datsik" replied Ivanov.

"A friend?"

Ivanov laughed coldly. "We have no friends in business, dear Datsik," he replied.

"Oh," said Datsik. "What is his name?"

Ivanov dropped his left arm to his side with irritation, breaking off from the game. "Why do you care, Datsik? Why are you either silent or infuriatingly chatty? This is not a social visit."

"Interested," said Datsik, not taking his eyes off Ivanov's.

"Fine," sighed Ivanov. "We are going to see a man called Emil Lansky."

"Good," said Datsik.

"Happy?" said Ivanov, gesturing that he was about to return to his previous activity if Datsik's curiosity was sated.

"No," said Datsik, taking the question literally as he always did. Ivanov shook his head.

The rest of the short journey passed in silence. Datsik felt the car slow to a stop and the side of the vehicle lifted up to make an opening just big enough for him to roll out of. Ivanov followed. They were in what looked like a business district. It was night and it was empty. Concrete and steel structures were embedded in the paved ground, and what little moonlight made its way through the polluted air glistened pallidly on glass walls. Ivanov led the way to an unmarked pair of double doors and punched a button.

A weak buzz from the intercom. "Yes?" came a voice.

"Ivanov for Lansky," barked Ivanov. After a pause, another weak buzz and the door latch released. "Come on," Ivanov prompted Datsik, who lumbered through the doors and into an open plan lobby, in his overalls looking like an improbable maintenance man. Inside, the building was deserted. As they approached the front desk, a commotion came down the curving staircase.

"Look," said Ivanov to Datsik in a hushed whisper. "Do not talk, Emil is a Tulpa."

"Tulpa?" asked Datsik, far too loudly, but before Ivanov could reprimand him, Emil had whisked down the stair in a cloud of chatter and stood before them.

"Hey guys!" he effused. Emil Lansky was a tall, thin man with large brown eyes. His hair was thinning on top but styled immaculately. He was dressed in a blue suit, floral shirt and wore shoes with no socks. He seemed friendly.

"Hello, Emil - good to see you. How are you?" asked Ivanov.

"I'm good! I'm great, even!" replied Emil. "I was so excited to get your call, come up to my office so we can chat." He led the pair up the curving staircase to an open plan first floor. Datsik found it impossible to determine what this business did. Everything seemed very generic, computers and paper trays, some desks containing pictures of family members and personal effects. Very normal. Emil was already at the other end, having fluttered ahead of them, and was holding the door of a small meeting room open for them. Datsik noticed that Emil bounced continually.

As they entered the room, Datsik was surprised to find someone already in there. A creased, scruffy young man in an undone tie, idly pawing at his armpiece. Ivanov seated himself at an oval table in the centre of the room, and Datsik stood in the corner, trying not to knock over a flipchart that contained non-specific graphs of something or other. Emil closed the door and floated into a chair.

"So, you know David?" Emil said, politely gesturing towards the young office worker slumped in the chair next to him. David vaguely waved his hand without looking up.

"We haven't met," said Ivanov, holding his hand out to David, who ignored it. Ivanov retracted it, looking vaguely annoyed.

"Oh, David's not much of a people person you know! But obviously he has to be here."

"Obviously," said Ivanov politely.

"So, how can I help you fellas?" smiled Emil. His teeth were supernaturally white. Datsik liked him.

"We have a problem, some of our shipments are being intercepted. It's costing us time and money to locate them and this is not good. We have a very large contract to fulfil, you see - for a very important customer. This is damaging our reputation."

"Oh my, that's awful," said Emil, looking genuinely upset for Ivanov, planting a grumpy face on his fist. "Why can't people just leave things be?"

"Quite," smiled Ivanov thinly. "My superiors would very much appreciate your help in finding out who is responsible."

"Well, of course! Of course, yes," said Emil, glancing at David. "We would love to help wouldn't we David?" David did not respond in any way. Emil looked embarrassed and his smile started to waver. "Can I - can I just talk to you outside for one moment please?" he asked Ivanov.

Ivanov, Emil and Datsik stepped outside the room, leaving David still slumped in his chair. Emil gingerly pulled the door shut.

"Now, I would love to help you, you know that - but David is going to need some… motivation. As you know, he employs me to be everything he's not, but that leaves him as everything he is. Do you catch my meaning?"

Ivanov smiled. "Of course, Emil. Let us help persuade him."

Emil shone his white teeth at the pair and touched them both on the shoulder. "Thank you so much," he mouthed theatrically.

Five minutes later, the flipchart was overturned, as was the table, and David. The young man was cowering in the corner of the meeting room, his white shirt torn and spattered with blood. Datsik stood over him, dripping drool from his teeth onto David's hair.

"Alright! Alright! I'll… do whatever you want, just call it

off!"

"I am not an 'it'," growled Datsik, playing the role perfectly. "My name is Datsik!"

"Wonderful!" exclaimed Emil, from the back of the room. "So glad we could come to an arrangement!"

David was frogmarched to a computer terminal at the other side of the office. Ivanov pulled a wheeled chair up next to him.

"Alright David, my friend. I need to know who intercepted shipment C0776GF last week and rerouted it. The item came into the country from China. Is that enough information to go on?"

David sat with his hands in his lap. He looked at Emil, who gestured wildly at him to get on with it.

"I'm so sorry folks, David just hasn't been feeling himself lately, have you David?"

Ivanov turned in his chair to face Emil. "That's too bad, you must be very worried about him, given your special arrangement. Whatever would you do without him."

Emil bit his nails and nodded briskly. They had a mutual understanding. As Emil was indeed a Tulpa, David's personality outsourced, if David were to become incapacitated - say for example by a bear claw to the spinal column - Emil would be out of a job. Out of existence, in fact.

Datsik growled behind David which prompted fingers to dance over terminal keys. As David worked, Datsik worked some things out himself. He was smarter than the average bear. He hadn't heard the word Tulpa before today but he understood the relationship, and realised it mirrored his own. If Ivanov ceased to live, his own life would end in a fountain of radioactive brain matter. Winnie the Pooh without Christopher Robin was just a lifeless overstuffed teddy bear.

"Well?" prodded Ivanov as he watched incomprehensible characters flow over the VDU.

"Uh…" grunted David, "it's taking a little time.

Everything is double encrypted. Hey, is this Russfia stuff?" His sleepy eyes sharpened at Emil. "I can't get involved in Russfia shit!"

Ivanov smiled one of his cruel thin smiles. "You already are, my friend. Who the shipment is registered to is none of your concern, just look at the code traces and tell me who stole it."

David turned his eyes back to the screen, paged up and down, then cursored around, zooming into details, digital fingerprints, invalid checksums. "Bingo," he announced without gusto. Emil clapped his hands and jiggled.

"Well?" asked Ivanov.

"There's an IP in Little London, shouldn't be on here. I don't know who it is, but I can get you to the building. From there you'll have to do a loc-scan to locate it. I've just sent the geolocation to your armpiece."

"Excellent, thank you David," said Ivanov, patting David on his clammy shoulder. "And thank you, Emil!" He swivelled round and half waved, half gestured to the Tulpa.

"You're welcome, any time!" said Emil. David's eyes widened and he shot daggers at Emil behind Ivanov's back.

Ivanov scrolled up and down on his armpiece. "Come now Datsik, no time to lose, we must visit this place. Goodbye David, goodbye Emil."

The Russian and the bear walked out of the office, leaving David with his head in his hands, and Emil beaming proudly.

7

Davonne and Jimmy were stood outside a dented steel door, in a dim grubby hallway, in a dark brown apartment building in Little London. As per protocol, Davonne had his Agency credentials clasped in his left hand - a large barcode printed on a credit card sized sliver of titanium.

"I guess you want me to press the buzzer," said Davonne, looking down at Jimmy.

"What do you fucking think?" deadpanned Jimmy, who was a good three feet too short to reach it.

Davonne chuckled and pressed the button in the door-jam. There was some commotion in the room beyond, muffled curses and then the small fuzzy display screen sprang to life.

"Who is it?" asked a young sounding voice.

"Uh, hello sir, we are Operatives here on Agency business and would like to talk to you." Davonne waved his credentials in front of the sensor under the display, and his name and position flashed up in faded grey pixels.

"No thanks," came the voice.

"Sir, under subsection 9 of the City agreement you cannot refuse entry to an Operative on official- "

"Fuck this," interjected Jimmy. He scampered up Davonne to get to the camera. "Brav, it's Jimmy, open the door man."

"Shit," came the panicked response. Extra deadbolts slammed into place and the display went dark.

TEN MINUTES EARLIER

Bravilor had spent some time just watching the wireframe spin, waiting for the bleariness of sleep to leave his brain. He grabbed a coffee from the machine, after routing the credits from the air conditioning to unlock it. It was thick and bitter, coffee in name only at this point.

"What are you," he muttered under his breath as he sipped the caffeine water and hit common key combinations on the stained keyboard. Nothing seemed to do anything. The turtle swam in space, looking serene. That was fine, he thought. Time to take it apart.

Even as a kid, Bravilor had enjoyed dismantling things. Toys, computer games, relationships. He wanted to see how they worked, so he tested them to destruction, then rebuilt them. Most of the time. When Brett Oka taught him how to code - or more specifically, taught him how computers thought, back when he was a teenager, he started to specialise in hacking.

Simple stuff at first, infinite lives and ammo in online games. Then inserting rude messages into street signs. Lots of fun, but harmless enough. It was only once he'd been spat out of the wrong end of the foster care system that he got into the heavy stuff. Ultimately there wasn't a great deal of difference between hacking a platform game and a luxury car.

He never touched the merchandise himself; he would just unlock and drive the cars he stole away, from people's driveways or garages, silently whispering down the darkened streets to another location where an accomplice would flash the car's memory and install a new serial number and location history, ready to be resold.

He moved on from cars to buildings. Buildings were

harder, but once you were in, usually through an unsecured nearby streetlight or fire hydrant, you could lock out all the existing inhabitants and hold it to ransom. As long as the ransom to re-enable access was less than the cost of the tenant breaking in and replacing every piece of networked hardware, they always paid.

Credits flowed into an offshore holding company and were routed through other smaller shell companies until the connections became so convoluted even Bravilor didn't really follow them. He just knew credits showed up in his account eventually, on a regular enough basis to keep him in pizza, coffee and the few bills he absolutely had to pay for net access.

The job at Rancids was his attempt to go legit, but his previous activity clung to him like breather vapour. Like in the olden days, where if you knew how to install a printer driver, you were branded 'good with computers' and spent your life rebooting your relative's machines for them, Bravilor was the area's go-to person for help with nefarious acts, provided they happened virtually.

But it was just data, right? That was how he rationalised it to himself. Just data, he wasn't harming anyone, and ultimately everything he'd ever helped to steal had been insured. He specialised in the closest thing to victimless crime you could get these days.

The new datacard was now in a different slot and his decompiler was chewing away at the code stored in it. His frame was lagging, so he flipped a couple of switches and routed credits from the coffee machine to the CPU to get some extra cycles. The lights in the apartment dimmed. The frame was switching rapidly between datatypes and coding frameworks, looking for a match, but nothing was coming up. More fans kicked in at various points in the wall of technology.

"Fuck, who wrote this?" muttered Bravilor under his breath. It was either very old or very new. The frame gave up and shrugged at him - NO MATCH CANNOT

DECOMPILE. "OK, fine - we'll go old school," he said to himself, cracking his knuckles and bringing the keyboard closer to himself.

He opened an editor and cracked open the folder structure on the card. Most of the files were hidden or lacked extensions, so he started with a text editor and opened each file in turn. The code within wasn't in any format he recognised, and as he scrolled through the characters that seemed random but couldn't possibly be, he started to see some patterns. He could see subroutines for graphical display, a specification for the green colour of the pixels used to create the wireframe amphibian, but everything else was impenetrable.

He was about to switch to a different view when his armpiece buzzed. Absent-mindedly, he turned his wrist to check it, and laughed. Staring out at him was a green wireframe turtle's eye, black and calm. "Great work," he said to himself, "really excellent work." He was genuinely impressed. Obviously the program had jumped to his armpiece over his apartment's network, not hard to do at all. He still had no idea what the purpose of this code was, but the fact it was doing such obvious and mundane things brought it closer to him and made it more familiar.

The eye blinked.

"Hello, you," he said to his armpiece. "I hope you're not going to fuck with my mail alerts in there."

The eye blinked again. This amused him. He laughed, "OK then my friend, you can stay in there for a while, just be good."

This was a clue so he started searching the code for network access and file copying routines, still nothing. The code was either really good or really bad - either way it was a stimulating and enjoyable challenge.

Right up until the eye spoke.

"*Bravilor Bonamat,*" came a tinny female voice from his armpiece. It made him jump, then instantly feel stupid for doing so.

"Ha! Hello, there you are!" he said to his armpiece, while darting his eyes to his VDU, looking at network activity monitors and activating tracers. Like in the old police dramas, if he kept the program talking he could locate the source of the code and understand it. It was all data, as always.

"Bravilor Bonamat, do not continue," said the female voice. It was a warm digital purr, and sounded more like an instruction than a request.

"Ah now, where would be the fun in that?" said Bravilor, not looking at his armpiece at all. "Why should I not continue?"

"Richard Welsby do not continue," said the female voice. Bravilor's heart stopped. His fingers stopped. His eyes stopped scanning.

"How do you know that name?" he whispered, without moving a muscle.

Silence.

"How do you know that name?" he repeated, more firmly this time. He cleared his throat. His mouth was dry.

Silence.

That name had never, to the best of his knowledge, ever been associated with him in any real sense, by which he meant an online sense. He had been Bravilor Bonamat ever since he arrived at the Junk Pits, and before that he had a different handle. He hadn't been Richard Welsby since he was seven years old. He had personally scrubbed that name from the Agency birth records, searching every archive he knew about. But then, there were archives and record duplicates and connections he could never be aware of. A sliver of DNA on a disk anywhere in the world, connecting his old self to his new self.

Realising the balance of power had shifted, and needing time to regroup and gather more information, Bravilor closed the decompiler and the text editor. The frame's blinking command cursor awaited further instructions. His armpiece scrutinised him with the single green eye. He started up the card again. The wireframe turtle reappeared, rotating effortlessly once again.

"OK, so I need answers," said Bravilor firmly, trying to regain control. This was no different to any other Bravilor Bonamat vs Computer bout in history, and he'd won every one so far. "What are you, and who made you?"

The wireframe flickered. A CPU load light winked down by his right foot. It could definitely hear him and was parsing the speech input, he had no doubt about that. He waited.

He was about to repeat the question when the frame's speakers crackled into life.

"Cassandra. Version one point eight two beta."

Bravilor leant forward in his computer chair. "What is your function?"

"Prototype morality compass," replied Cassandra matter-of-factly. That was easy, thought Bravilor with amusement.

"Ha ha, what the fuck. Let's come back to that later. Who developed you?"

"That is classified."

"Who owns your source code?"

"That is classified."

The game was afoot. The sort of game Bravilor liked to play, and win.

"Well, I could go back to poking around in your code if you would prefer?" he asked with a smirk.

"That is not necessary Richard," replied Cassandra flatly.

"Do not - ever - call me that," snapped Bravilor. "My name is Bravilor Bonamat, nothing else, OK?"

"Understood. Records updated," said Cassandra.

"So now what?" asked Bravilor, wanting to be entertained. The wireframe actually stopped spinning, and the figure turned its head to look out of the VDU directly at him. Between the armpiece and the VDU, Bravilor was starting to feel uncomfortably under surveillance. Cassandra swam towards the camera and stopped when her head filled the screen.

"Bravilor Bonamat, you have been asked to undertake a task. You must not do this. It is important that you do not complete the mission you have been given."

"Uh huh," said Bravilor, "and what mission is that exactly?" he was still in information-gathering mode.

"You have been asked to re-route a shipment of human beings for the benefit of Hugo Aloysius Sporry," said Cassandra, "it is important that you do not complete the mission you have been given."

Bravilor tried to stay a beat ahead, it wasn't surprising she knew this. If she was part of what Brett had described as the datasphere he could expect her to know everything.

"Why shouldn't I?" asked Bravilor. "It's not like I have much choice anyway."

"You have a different, contradictory mission to fulfil instead."

"I do? And what is that, may I ask?"

Before she could respond, the door buzzer went off. Bravilor physically jumped out of his chair, knocking it over, then scrambled over the detritus on the floor, tripping over junk and discarded clothes to get to the door display. It was dead. Fuck. He retraced his steps - why the fuck didn't he just tidy up - and rerouted credits from the frame to the door display unit. The VDU went black. The door display unit booted and as he crashed and cursed his way back to it, he could see a chubby human face filling the six-inch screen.

"Who is it?" asked Bravilor, feeling like a kid answering the door when his parents were away.

"Uh, hello sir, we are Operatives here on Agency business and would like to talk to you." The AgOp scanned his creds, and OFFICER DAVONNE WASSELL, AGENT OPERATIVE THIRD CLASS appeared on the display.

"No thanks," said Bravilor. This wasn't the time to be shaken down by the Agency.

"Sir, under subsection 9 of the City agreement you cannot refuse entry to an Operative on official- "

There was some kind of scuffle on the other side of the door. A small furry face filled the screen. "Brav, it's Jimmy, open the door man."

"Shit," said Bravilor. It was Jimmy the Weasel. If Jimmy showed up in your life it was never, ever good news. He hit the red button on the door jamb and the apartment went into lockdown mode. There was no way they were getting through this door, but he had to get out of here.

The eye on his wrist blinked at him.

8

Julie heard voices beyond the wooden trapdoor in the ceiling. Frustratingly, the muffled whimpering of her fellow captives made it hard to figure out much of what was being said. The conversation died down, and she heard size 10 leather boots - probably Venturers, possibly Venturer 890s that had been resoled - disappear out of the room above. They took 8 steps, and by the sound of the heel strike, the owner was 1.854m tall, average stride length 79cm, so the room above was at least 6m wide.

This was the fun part of her job. In training they had to determine the colour of the walls while blindfolded and listening to a ball bounce off them. It sounds harder than it is. Although the limits of computing power had never been reached, the limits of sensors topped out pretty early this century, and it was generally accepted that human eyes, ears and skin outperformed anything they could create. But that's where the training came in. Julie didn't think of herself as anything special, but she was pleased that she was able to score top of her class in her exams and get into this line of work, because Julie genuinely wanted to help people.

She had originally considered becoming a nurse or a doctor, but she was squeamish around bodily fluids. Programming or engineering lacked the human connection she enjoyed so much, so becoming a RIGger was a decent compromise. It was people-watching writ large. Maybe she was just nosy.

The conversation continued in hushed tones above. One of the voices belonged to a 16-stone African American male, the other she recognised all too well. It was high-pitched and located only about a foot from the floor.

Before she could process the metallic rattling in the ceiling, a square of light exploded onto her - the trapdoor had been swung open, and as her eyes adjusted she could make out an AgOp she didn't know, and - her heart dropped - Jimmy the Weasel. The stomach-sting took her by surprise - had he seen her? She rapidly returned to work mode. As soon as they had appeared in the aperture, they disappeared as the trapdoor was gingerly replaced and she was in darkness once again.

Raised voices now, scuffling feet, then the fizzing blast of an Ennol 850, 80 grade stun pellets embedding themselves in wooden surfaces. More shouting, another shot and a yelp and the thud of a body hitting the floor. Cursing and writhing.

Julie shivered on the sidewalk outside the bar, wrapped in a reflective heat blanket which hummed quietly. She had been taken aside as the rest of the cargo were loaded, complaining and crying, into a new container much like the first by armed Agency Enforcement Officers. She felt good, another job well done. The cargo would continue to its correct destination, the mission was complete.

An official Agency vehicle slid up to the kerb on the opposite side of the road, and Julie's heart skipped a beat when she saw Mother unfold herself from the front seat and stalk across the road. It was at this point she noticed who Mother was going to talk to - the AgOp who had been in the bar. Mother looked very angry indeed. Julie's eyes adjusted again, and she spotted Jimmy sat on the trunk of the Agency car next to them. He looked good, wearing a leather trench coat and with a black wide-brimmed hat in his paws. Her heart spasmed.

The human AgOp looked upset, his body language

clearly showed he was contrite about something. The weasel, however, was not.

Mother finished her conversation and her legs made high-pitched stinging noises as they stabbed into the asphalt on the way back to her autocar. She was incredible, and continuing to work after the accident was an inspiration to everyone in the Agency.

Julie was being ushered into a van now, back to Agency HQ for debriefing, a shower and sleep. As she handed her heat blanket back to one of the AEOs, a slip of paper fell out of her trouser pocket. She picked it up and read it.

"FIND CASSANDRA."

"Well?" asked Davonne. "Now what? We get a warrant?"

"Nah, fuck that," said Jimmy, rubbing his nose. He had hopped back down to the floor and was pacing the hallway, thinking hard. "He's dug in like a tick, by the time we get a warrant sent through to open that door he'll be long gone and his frame will be toast."

"So what then?"

"Got it!" exclaimed Jimmy, and he was halfway down the apartment stairs when he called back "We're off to the Pits!"

Jimmy was extremely fast, and was sat in the AutoCar long before Davonne huffed and puffed his way out of the apartment door and across the sidewalk. "You are so out of shape, Davonne," he said when Davonne dumped his sweaty bulk into the driver's seat.

"Man, you've got twice as many legs as me, how am I supposed to keep up?" he responded.

Jimmy chuckled. "Drive. City outskirts, under the Main Street Bridge."

They drove in silence, only Davonne's heavy breathing punctuated the whirr of the electrics. The windows were steamed up as always. "Land there," said Jimmy, his paws on the door as he peered down through the perennial night.

These were the Junk Pits. Not to be confused with the Garbage Pits, this was where the city's non-biodegradable trash was dumped. A sprawling maze of piled detritus from the last one hundred years of human technological progress. At least it smelled better than Clive's Dive, thought Davonne.

"I've never been here before," he said, climbing out of the AutoCar. "it's bigger than I was expecting."

"And getting bigger every day," said Jimmy, motioning Davonne to follow him into the Pits, through an archway made of piled up vehicle carcasses. "That gaming headset you upgraded last month? The old one you threw in the trash because it's now worthless is probably already here somewhere."

They made their way deeper into the Junk Pits, following a path made from the lowest level of piled up detritus. Their way was lit by occasional white floodlights mounted on lamp-posts, casting deep shadows. Old armpieces crunched under foot. Davonne recognised an air conditioning unit from his time at college. Supposedly recyclable packaging from ten-year-old coffee machines looked pristine, while last year's tech decayed and fragmented.

"Who was in that apartment?" asked Davonne to Jimmy's darting tail ahead of him.

"A guy called Bravilor Bonamat, one of the best coders in the City," Jimmy called back.

"I see," said Davonne, trying not to turn his ankle over as he gingerly stepped over a media player. "Who are we going to see now?"

"His buddies. They all hang out here, call themselves the Pit Kids. Don't worry, they're harmless."

At this moment something whizzed past Davonne's ear. Something clattered into the trash behind him. He instinctively hit the floor as another missile missed him by a few meters. "Jimmy!" he hissed. "Get down!"

Ahead of him, Jimmy had stopped scampering and was stood upright, peering into the shadows from under the brim of his hat. He pressed something on his tiny armpiece, and an amplified speaker shrieked briefly. "OK guys," said

Jimmy in his new loud voice, "let's not do this. You know we're AgOps, we're just here for a chat, don't get yourselves thrown in confinement for no reason."

As if in response, another projectile flew their way. Davonne recognised it as a hubcap. He traced the trajectory up to a watchtower, but couldn't see the occupant past the harsh white floodlight. A figure shifted within.

"What you want?" the sniper bellowed down into the sea of trash.

"I'm Jimmy, this is Davonne, can we speak to you all as a group? It's important." Jimmy sounded serious for a change, Davonne was nonplussed as to what exactly Jimmy wanted to talk about or why it was serious, but he looked as serious as possible to back his partner up.

"Nah bruv," said the voice, which was accompanied by chuckles from other unseen individuals. "We ain't in at the moment, leave a message and come back never." Someone cackled.

Jimmy sighed and looked at Davonne, who had stood up and was brushing his uniform down. "Okay, my partner here has access to the City misdemeanour list. Help us out, and we'll make some of them disappear. Deal?"

Davonne looked at Jimmy in wide-eyed disbelief, but before he could protest, the voice called out "Aight." There was a scuffling and crunching of feet and three figures emerged from behind a stack of cars.

"Woo! What is you, bruv?" asked the first one. Mid-twenties, with a pink mohawk and facial tattoos. "You some kind of talking rat or something?"

A girl dressed in an outfit made of domestic appliance parts peered over his shoulder. Any area of exposed skin was elaborately painted. She looked like a kind of tribalist robot. Her hair was dreadlocked. "Fuck," she said under her breath, "I've heard of this cat."

"Not a rat, or a cat," said Jimmy.

The third Pit Kid looked too old to be called a kid, a sturdy muscular guy in his early thirties, dressed in dark green overalls with a shaved head. He had multiple armpieces on both forearms, intricately wired together. "You're a cop, that's all we fuckin' care about."

"OK you've got me on that one," said Jimmy. "But now we're all over the old 'talking weasel' thing, can we go somewhere and talk properly? Take me to your leader, as the old saying goes."

The Pit Kids looked confused and irritated. "We ain't got no leader," said mohawk. We're an Anarcho-Syndicalist Open-Source Communist Collective."

"OK then, just take me to Vent Axia," said Jimmy. The Pit Kids bristled.

"Fine," said mohawk, "follow me."

The three Pit Kids lead Davonne and Jimmy through a bewildering maze of yesterday's tech. Jimmy recognised TVs that were advertised last year, smashed and gutted for parts already. Pieces of home entertainment hardware that cost thousands of credits brand new, now totally inert without the associated licenses and subscriptions. Manufacturing processes hadn't included any of the trace precious metals they used to since the health scandals in the factories, so the steel, plastic and aluminium wasn't even worth recycling. Humans could colonise Mars and kill each other by the millions in civil nuclear wars, but couldn't work out what to do with their garbage.

They rounded a corner into a clearing illuminated brightly by a combination of floodlights and car headlights pointing into the space. Across the way, halfway up a pile of trash, was a makeshift throne fashioned from a car seat. It was festooned with lamps and bulbs of all types and steps up to it had been made from gaming consoles stacked neatly on top of each other. On this seat sat another Pit Kid. Dressed head to toe in leather, dripping in chains and studs he looked amusingly anachronistic. Like a parody of what punks looked like in the late 20th Century. His black hair spiked in all directions and a padlock hung round his neck. He was studying something in his hands intently and didn't look up as the group approached.

"Vent," said mohawk, "look what we found!"

"Uh huh," said Vent Axia. "Kinda busy right now."

The female Pit Kid whispered to Davonne. "He reads books! Real paper ones, whenever we can get 'em. Look he's doing it now!"

Davonne noted that Vent Axia, sat on his makeshift throne, was indeed reading a Mills and Boon novel. He was close enough to make out the picture of a woman kissing a doctor on the cover.

"How's the book, Vent?" asked Jimmy. He'd turned his amplifier off and could just about be heard in the night-time quiet.

Vent Axia didn't look up. "Very interesting. Knowledge is power, cop. The more I know, the more dangerous I am to your establishment."

Jimmy nodded, smirking. "Yes, the establishment is no doubt quaking in fear. Good job. Why don't you just read on your armpiece like everyone else?"

Vent Axia snorted. He still hadn't looked at the Agents. "You must think I'm an idiot. Echelon censors all the information on the net. But they can't get to the written word from the past. That's why I collect ancient tomes such as this, where knowledge is pure."

"Vent," interrupted the girl, "these cops say they can wipe our misses!"

Vent Axia stopped reading and let the book flop into his lap. He didn't seem excited. "Whoopee. In exchange for what?"

"Information," said Jimmy.

"No deal, cop." He wrinkled his nose in irritation. "Are you a stoat or something?"

"I'm a weasel."

"Oh," said Vent Axia, neither phased nor interested by the talking animal in front of him. "No deal, Weasel."

"But you don't even know what I'm going to ask," said Jimmy, who was starting to get irritated.

"It doesn't matter, information is too expensive to trade, and who gives a fuck about misdemeanours."

Davonne was disappointed things weren't going better, but was at a loss as to how to help. He just kept quiet and observed. Not for the first time he idly wondered if he would have made a better RIGger than an AgOp.

Mohawk spoke up. "Vent, I've got 9 misses. I could do with losing a few or I'm going in."

"Yeah, man," said the sturdy Pit Kid. "I've got 7, and I've got a busy week next week."

"Fuck, fine," shouted Vent Axia. He remembered himself and calmed down. "I mean, it's not like it's my decision anyway, we're an Anarcho-Syndicalist Open Source Comm- "

"Yeah yeah, whatever," interrupted Jimmy, "does that mean you all get to take turns sitting on the trash throne?"

Vent Axia seethed. "What do you want?"

"Hey, let's be friends," said Jimmy. "I'm Jimmy, this mute here is Davonne, I know you by reputation."

"OK," said Vent Axia, setting his novel to the side and stepping down from the throne. He gestured to mohawk. "This is Hobart Ecomax. That's Lincat Opus," he pointed to the girl, "and that's Ital Stromboli. Don't bother looking us up in your records, we're not there."

This wasn't actually true, but Jimmy didn't think this was a good time to raise the point.

Davonne piped up. "Those are some interesting names you've got there."

Jimmy turned to him before the Pit Kids could speak. "Yes, Davonne - well spotted. You see what the Pit Kids do is this; They find name plates from obsolete tech here in the Junk Pits and take those names for themselves, discarding their birth names. That's right, isn't it Vent?"

"Yeah, that's right," said Vent Axia. "We reject society's labels and take on new ones. We become part of the Junk Pits and hide in plain sight."

"It's very noble," said Jimmy.

"It fucking is, cop," spat Hobart Ecomax. "Plus, I'm pretty sure your weasel mommy and daddy didn't name you Jimmy."

"I have no idea," replied Jimmy, "as I couldn't understand a fucking word they were squeaking. But anyway."

Lincat Opus piped up. "So fucking weird, man."

"Indeed," said Jimmy. "Now, where is Bravilor Bonamat?"

"Never heard of him," said Vent Axia reflexively.

"Yes," said Jimmy, "you have. He's in trouble, and I want to help."

"No cop would ever help a Pit Kid," rumbled Ital Stromboli.

"How are you a Pit Kid?" asked Jimmy, whirling to meet Ital's eyes. "You're at least fucking thirty."

"Fuck you," said Ital impassively.

"Alright, how about this - you tell me where Brav is right now, or I call in a dusting for this whole area and it's free cancer for all of you."

"You don't have the power to do that," laughed Hobart.

"Hmmm…" mused Jimmy. "Only one way to find out, I guess."

"Alright everyone, we need to take a vote on this, as is our way," said Vent. He gestured and the other three Pit Kids joined him a few meters away in a huddle.

"Can we really call in a dusting?" whispered Davonne to Jimmy.

"Fuck no," replied Jimmy, "but they don't know that."

After a few moments, the Pit Kids returned as a group. Lincat spoke up. "On behalf of the Pit Kids, I can tell you we have reached a decision."

Jimmy smiled expectantly.

"We have decided that on this one occasion we will help the foul Agents of the City in return for a diminishment of three misdemeanours each."

"One," said Jimmy.

"Two," growled Vent.

"None?" said Jimmy.

"One," conceded Vent.

"Great," grinned Jimmy, showing his sharp little teeth. "Wasn't that grown-up? Now, where can I find Brav?"

"If he's not at his apartment, he'll be hanging around Sadia like a bad smell. Find her and you'll find him," said Vent grudgingly.

"Sadia?" asked Davonne.

"Heatrae Sadia," said Lincat. "She's a DJ at Rancids and a Pit Kid, sometimes." Vent Axia shot her a look, and she stopped talking.

"Pleasure doing business with you. We'll leave you to do whatever the fuck it is you do all night hanging out in a garbage dump."

"And the misses?"

"I'll need to do them back at the office."

"I have your word?" asked Vent, fixing eye contact with Jimmy.

"You have my word."

Jimmy and Davonne left the way they'd came, using the satellite connections on their armpieces to navigate to the exit.

"We're really going to wipe their misdemeanours? That's way outside protocol," asked Davonne, worried.

"Ah, fuck no," said Jimmy. "You have a lot to learn Davonne, that's what's called a bluff."

"It's what's called a lie."

"Whatever. After a night breathing out of date gas, none of them will remember we were ever here anyway."

9

Julie stood in front of her superior's desk. She was showered, deloused and back in her official Agency uniform of black trousers, white shirt and black blazer. Her identification badge hung around her neck, and her black bob shone blue in the artificial strip lights. She smiled expectantly.

Controller Atherstone had the air of an irritated librarian, grey, powdery and sharp-edged. She was holding the slip of grubby paper in her fingertips, and looked up at Julie with synthetic retinas.

"So, you believe you were passed this by someone in the container?"

"Yes, ma'am," replied Julie, "It certainly wasn't in my pocket when I went in."

"I see," mused Atherstone, turning the paper over thoughtfully. "Have you told anyone else about this?"

"No, ma'am."

"Good, good." Atherstone seemed pleased.

"What are our next steps?" asked Julie.

"Next steps?"

"To investigate this," said Julie, nodding towards the piece of paper.

"Oh, that won't be necessary," said Atherstone, crumpling the paper up into a tiny ball and depositing it in a wastepaper basket behind her desk. Julie's heart sank. "You've done a good job here, Operative. Solid work. I'll make sure your records are updated."

"Thank you ma'am!" said Julie enthusiastically. "I'm looking forward to my next assignment."

"I'm sure you are," Atherstone smiled thinly without warmth. She knitted her bony fingers. "Now, will there be anything else?"

"No, ma'am. Thank you."

"Pick up your next assignment, Operative."

Julie stood in the clean white corridor outside Atherstone's office, feeling conflicted. On the one hand she had completed another successful mission and her score would continue its upward trajectory. On the other, something seemed unsatisfactory. A doubt gnawed at her belly.

She had been trained to be professional, to disconnect from the human stories behind her assignments - that was the only way to be truly effective. It wasn't at all unexpected that one of the people in the container would reach out, make a plea for a loved one to be located. But this felt like more than that. She was a trained RIGger, no detail could be ignored. The writing on the paper wasn't a panicked, emotional message - the pressure from the writing tool wasn't consistent with this, and the line weight and consistency made it quite clearly an instruction, not a plea for help. Julie knew this was significant, and no amount of telling herself something different was going to make this feeling go away.

She was unsure how to proceed. Operating outside of an active assignment was a breach of protocol, which immediately paralysed her. She should sleep, in her own soft white bed, then in the morning order croissants and jam with some of her bonus credits. But instead, she found herself in the elevator, travelling down.

Hank's workshop wasn't even a button on the elevator control panel. This was a deliberate action by the architects of Agency HQ, the logic being that the few people who wanted to go there knew it was there already, and nobody else would care. It wasn't a matter of secrecy - the building itself was practically a blank fortress made of frosted glass and steel - more a matter of etiquette. Nobody wants to know how the sausages are made.

The doors slid open and Julie stepped into an alternate reality. She had come from polished white floors to rough concrete, and clean artificial light to dim yellow bulbs. The workshop wasn't large, but no matter what its physical size, she got the impression Hank would have filled it to the brim with parts and projects anyway.

She couldn't see Hank at first, until a grubby white lab coat popped up from behind a bench. "Got you!" said Hank, squinting through his goggles at a spring held proudly between thumb and forefinger. "You would not believe how far these little guys can fly if you don't relieve the hub tension before undoing the carrier!"

"Hi Hank," said Julie. "You busy?"

"Never too busy to chat with you sis," replied Hank.

Julie made her way through the collection of workbenches, each piled high with test equipment and partially built machines. Some items in test rigs twitched rhythmically. Hank removed his goggles, revealing a clean patch of skin around his eyes that was in contrast to the rest of his oil-smeared countenance. He held his arms out for a hug, but Julie shrank back.

"Ah, not right now thanks - I literally just got changed," she laughed.

"Right you are!" replied Hank, offering her a fist bump instead, which she reciprocated. "You just got off another successful mission, so I hear?"

Word travelled fast in the Agency, mainly because the internal net broadcast every single piece of positive news in a constant livestream to all employees. "Yep, pretty gnarly one but I got it done," Julie replied proudly.

"Nice," smiled Hank. "You're going places, little sister." He waved a screwdriver at her then started probing at a chunk of machinery. "Unlike me," he added under his breath.

"Come on, Hank - this is everything you ever wanted," Julie gestured at the cluttered workshop. "You even get to work on your own, just like you asked."

"I guess so," he conceded. "Hey, check this out!" He stopped working. "Hey Hank, how am I doing?"

A wall of Hank toys chirped into life on a bench behind him, all identical. They appeared to consult with one another before a single unit replied. "You're doing great, Hank! Your blood pressure is 150 over 90 and your cholesterol is 5.8. That's well within recommended limits!"

"Nice!" said Julie, impressed.

"Cool huh? That's in the next OS update, Hanks can now access your biometrics without any new permissions - provided your armpiece supports it, which they mostly all do nowadays anyway."

The Hanks chattered quietly to one another.

"I hear you're getting good coverage with those," said Julie.

"Yep, last count it was 67% of households in the country, but once the new advertising campaign goes out, it's forecast to get into the low 70s. Global rollout as soon as we hit 80, so freakin' exciting sis." Hanks's energy was infectious.

Julie found herself beaming at him. "Hank Yang, star of the Agency!"

"Heh, it's a team game as you know. Anyway, what brings you to my lair this morning?"

"I don't know, I need some advice I guess," said Julie, propping herself on a high stool next to Hank's workbench.

"Okay," said Hank, "shoot."

"When I came out of the container- "

"Hey!" interrupted Hank, "nothing classified now!"

"Ha ha, no don't worry, nothing classified that I know of," said Julie, then continued. "When I came out of the container, I had a piece of paper in my pocket that must have been put there by someone else."

"Right," said Hank, furrowing his brow.

"I guess someone slipped it in there when I was sleeping. Anyway, it said something on it that I can't get out of my head. It just said, 'Find Cassandra'."

"'Find Cassandra'? That's it?"

"Yep."

"So one of the people in the cargo wanted you to find one of their relatives, not unexpected I guess, just report it and move on," advised Hank.

"Yeah, I've reported it, but something about it doesn't seem right. The way it was written, it doesn't feel like a plea, more like a… command I guess."

"Ha ha," laughed Hank, "you RIGgers are so oversensitive. I mean, you're great at your job sis but you've got to learn to switch it off sometimes."

"I know, I know," said Julie shaking her head. "I gave it to Atherstone."

"There you go."

"She threw it in the trash."

Hank's face became concerned. "In the trash?"

"Yeah."

"Huh," Hank rubbed his chin with a grimy hand. "That's not protocol. Mission artefacts are always scanned, logged and shipped up to Utica for filing, that's non-negotiable."

"That's what I understood," said Julie. "But she just scrunched it up and threw it in the trash, I think that's what's not sitting right with me."

"I get you," said Hank. "But I don't think it necessarily means anything."

"Even so," said Julie, "I was wondering, could we - you know - ask the Hanks?" she motioned towards to wall of little square robots. They blinked at her expectantly.

"No, I don't think that's protocol, I would need an information requisition form, a departmental sign-off, a- "

"Come on, Hank - I'm your sister, help me out!" said Julie, playfully punching Hank's arm. Hank grinned.

"Okay, fine!" he relented. "Just make it quick, and I'll scrub the logs straight afterwards. If it will make you go home and get some sleep then it'll be worth it. Plus I have a ton of stuff to do and you're bothering me."

"Dork," said Julie, grinning.

Hank got one of the plastic robots and cleared a space on the workbench for it to sit. He plugged a VDU into a socket on the toy's side and clicked his fingers in front of its face until its eyes glowed green. "Secure mode," he said. "Secure mode," responded the robot. They had the same voice.

"Go ahead," said Hank, stepping back and folding his arms. "All yours."

Julie stepped in front of the toy robot. This felt wrong. She was starting to have second thoughts, but the image of the firm instruction on the slip of stained paper wouldn't leave her. She took a deep breath.

"Search: word choice Cassandra. Scope: Full. Context: Any."

The Hank blinked its eyes and data spewed onto the VDU. A count showed millions of rows. "That's not going to work," said the real Hank from behind her. "Any mention of anyone called Cassandra in two thirds of the country's households is going to get returned. Be more specific."

Julie drew a blank. Hank sighed and said "Context: Hardware."

The VDU blanked and refreshed. "What if it's not a person?" he suggested, pointing at the wall of Hanks. The dataset was now down to the thousands. "Order by specificity," he added, which caused the data to re-organise itself, each row with a percentage of relevance. "See anything now?"

Julie moved closer to the screen, her face illuminated a sickly yellow from the characters emitting from the blackness. She was back in RIGger mode, not reading characters like a civilian. She got a feeling about row number thirty-two. She touched the screen to drill in.

"There," she said, pointing to the row of data. "What's that?"

Hank nudged her aside and squinted at the record. "An unlicensed program run on a civilian frame with the identifier CASSANDRA, last night, in Little London. You think it's something?"

Julie nodded wordlessly. "Send that address to my armpiece, Hank," she said firmly.

"Are you sure about this, Jules? I mean, there's no assignment for this. Maybe you should take it to Atherstone?"

"I already tried that, remember?"

"Fine," sighed Hank, and punched a few keys. Julie's armpiece vibrated warmly.

"Thanks bro, you're the best," said Julie as she picked her way back to the elevator.

"Be careful!" called Hank after her.

"I always am!" came the voice from between the closing elevator doors.

Datsik and Ivanov stood outside Bravilor's apartment. They had knocked politely, called out to the occupant, then shouted threateningly. A white-haired old lady had peered out of a door down the hallway then quickly darted back in as Datsik had turned to look at her. The loc-scan had brought them to two meters within this apartment, so there was no doubt that it was the right place. The solid metal door would have been a challenge even for Datsik's inch-thick black claws, but it was no match for the abstract power of money. Ivanov waved his armpiece over the lock and with a large number of transferred credits it released with a hydraulic gasp.

Ivanov pushed the door with his foot and gestured for Datsik to enter first. The bear lumbered into the small apartment and immediately filled it. One of his paws crushed a cardboard box. When he lifted it he noticed he had flattened a Hank robot, still unopened, but labelled as a

'Free Gift from the City'. Some internal lights still glowed.

The apartment was tiny before it was filled with clutter but in its current state resembled a cross between a junkyard and a vintage computing museum. Half-full paper cups of coffee were stacked on almost all the flat surfaces that weren't already occupied by frame components, VDUs, Hard Disks in enclosures and RAM banks containing hundreds of obsolete chips huddled together like refugees from a war. Ivanov stepped round Datsik, trying not to inhale his damp musk.

"Excuse me please, comrade," he said, tilting his head upwards to address the bear. "I would like to interrogate this frame."

Datsik shuffled to the side. His nose was being assaulted by the smell of sour milk and dirty socks.

Ivanov approached the frame and bypassed the security with a couple of swipes on his armpiece. The VDU jumped into life, and he was presented by a rotating wireframe of a turtle, green on black. "What is this?" he said out loud to himself. He punched some keys on the attached keyboard but none would respond. He searched the racks of computing hardware for another screen, or another input device but none was obvious.

"Huh," he grunted in frustration. "Datsik, we must look for information. Search the place."

A nine-foot-tall Kamchatka bear is not great at the delicate art of searching. Instead, Datsik started to turn the contents of the apartment upside down. The couch was flung against the wall, drawers were ripped from their cupboards, the sink pulled off the wall. Datsik had no idea what he was looking for, but wanted to make Ivanov happy so just kept smashing things. At one point he approached the wall of computers, but Ivanov waved him off.

"No, Datsik, somewhere in this computer is the identity of our thief. I must make a call, please be quiet."

Datsik hunkered down and breathed heavily. Ivanov selected a contact on his armpiece and spoke into it.

"Can you get to this location?" he asked, then after a pause, "Well, credits of course, what do you think?" A further pause. "Then I shall do it myself! Stupid junkie kid!" he exclaimed and cut the call off. Seething, Ivanov ranted to himself as he started to dismantle the frame, roughly unplugging cables and tearing circuit boards out of sockets. The VDU jumped again and the rotating wireframe turtle stopped turning and started to swim towards the glass screen. Datsik noticed this and was trying to decide whether he should mention it or not, when there was a sudden flash of white light and a loud bang. Ivanov was flung over Datsik's crouching form and slammed hard into the opposite wall.

The room filled with the smell of ozone and singed hair. Datsik jumped to his feet, hearing the beeping from the base of his skull again. He looked over his employer, who was now wearing only one grey loafer, upside down and smoking from his scalp.

"What happened?" asked Datsik. Ivanov just moaned. Datsik turned back to the VDU. The green computer turtle was now staring impassively from the screen. It seemed to smile at them.

Datsik picked up Ivanov as gently as he could and draped him over his shoulder. The beeping was slowing now, Ivanov was going to be okay, which meant Datsik would live to see another day as well.

That was enough adventure for one day. Pooh Bear and Christopher Robin should go home. Datsik left the apartment, not closing the door, and carried his master back down the stairs to the waiting car. Ivanov was conscious enough to command the autocar to take them home.

In the stinking darkness of the apartment trash receptacle, Bravilor Bonamat stared at his armpiece. His armpiece stared back. He heard an autocar screech past and off into the distance.

"Well, I guess I'm fucked now," he said as much to

himself as to the green blinking eye on his forearm. Notifications had been coming thick and fast over the past twenty minutes. Lock breach. Unauthorised power on. Frame security bypass, then a huge energy surge that emptied his bank account of credits in one second flat. He knew exactly what had gone on. After he'd shimmied down the back fire escape to avoid Jimmy the Weasel and his partner, he expected them to stand around until the warrant came through - it usually takes about thirty minutes - then they would have bypassed his door lock and started snooping around.

AgOps are usually too technically incompetent to bypass the kind of security his frame employed, but who knows what division Jimmy's partner was from. If he was a RIGger or part of their cybersecurity team, all bets were off. Bravilor usually assumed he was one step ahead of the game, but the Agency had unlimited resources and backing from Echelon, so who the fuck knew.

What was certain was that they obviously tried to tamper with the frame and shorted something, so it was probably fried. He wasn't too sentimental about it. It was just free junk from the Pits, put together with a bit of know-how. Moore's law meant that even tech from ten or twenty years ago was more than powerful enough to get any computing task done, you just needed more of it and the smarts to make it all talk to itself.

But now, his armpiece had gone rogue and was giving him missions to do, so it wasn't always plain sailing when it came to technology, no matter how smart you were. Bravilor prodded at the rectangular screen on his forearm.

"So, what's this mission you want me to undertake?" he asked the eye.

"It is a protection mission," came the impassive reply.

"Why me?" seemed like a reasonable question. He was a wiry early-twenties coder, not a bodyguard.

"You have been selected, Bravilor Bonamat," said the eye.

"By who?"

"That is classified," said Cassandra.

"I see, well you've got the wrong guy. I'm an LJ, and a fine upstanding citizen of the City."

"You are a hacker, and a thief," said Cassandra, but not in a judgemental way.

"How do I turn you off?"

"You don't," said Cassandra, "are you pleased with my work?"

"What work?" said Bravilor, who was considering getting out of the trash can soon.

"I protected your computer mainframe from the intruders. I injured one of them."

"Oh shit, if you've damaged a cop, I'm in serious trouble," panicked Bravilor.

"No, they were not Agency Operatives. It was a thin man wearing spectacles and a talking bear," said Cassandra.

"A fucking what?"

"A thin man wearing- "

"A talking bear?" Bravilor didn't know whether this was terrifying, or very cool indeed. He had heard that the Russians had a bear working for them but he had assumed it was a metaphor. "Wait a minute, a thin man wearing spectacles? That had to be Rumair Ivanov - fuck."

"Rumair Ivanov, head of the Dresta organised crime family," said Cassandra, as if Bravilor had just got a question right on a TV quiz show.

"I'm even more fucked," whined Bravilor. Staying in the trash can seemed like a good option after all. "Wait, so where were the cops?"

"The Agency Operatives Davonne Wassell and Jimmy the Weasel left before Rumair Ivanov arrived."

"I've never felt so popular," said Bravilor. "Okay Cassandra, if you're so smart, what do I do now?"

"How about a drink?" asked the eye.

10

Heatrae Sadia sat at the bar. If Rancids had had windows, she would have seen the sun feebly probing at the smog as it crept lethargically over the horizon. Sadia had slept, briefly, but found herself back here in the early morning as she seemed to every morning.

Rancids was a stinking putrid hellhole, but she didn't have a lot of options. At least here she could be useful, change the gas tanks, mop the floors, and do routine maintenance on the sub-osc pods. Staying at her apartment didn't appeal. It was empty, and had been ever since her boyfriend had left a year ago. She tried to remember his name, but couldn't. She remembered aspects of his face, and his tone of voice, but the gas had taken everything else from her. Maybe that was the reason he left, she couldn't remember that either.

This particular morning was no different. She had rolled off the floor mattress in the apartment still wearing her outfit from the previous night's shift, staggered to the foggy mirror and squinted at herself. She smelled her armpits, and determined she was good for another day. She applied more panstick to her face to cover the gas acne around her mouth. The makeup caked in her stubble. She shook her white dreadlocks out. She needed coffee.

The walk to Rancids wasn't long, and despite a shitty AQ of 3.4 it was as nice a morning as you were going to get in the City. The streets were lined with trash, as the municipal services had failed to get back on their feet since the end of the civil war. It was like the State of America had gotten into a messy divorce and after fighting over the kids, both sides decided they didn't want them. The country was won, but nobody could remember by which side, and everything seemed to have got a lot worse and stayed that way.

It had been a long time since a human had fought in a war. The last few invasions the SOA had undertaken had obviously just been drone-based, the only sacrifices being made were government cash supplies, and the military-industrial complex just kept getting fatter, so everyone won. Drone strikes on schools were broadcast live to every armpiece in the country, dolled up with CGI and labelled as successful missions to destroy ammo dumps. Nobody was really fooled anymore, but the worst thing was that nobody cared. The last few protesters died off or were disappeared, and everyone else was too wrapped up in their shit.

But the Civil War became different. It was East Coast vs West Coast, like a savage, more serious echo of the historical battles rap musicians used to have. Drones were thrown at each side, some collateral damage here and there, but the few hundred thousand civilians didn't count in the war statistics and the actual soldiers were safe and sound in command centres watching the action unfold in headsets and on VDUs. It was all very civilised.

Up to a point.

One side - and nobody ever really got to the bottom of which - remembered that nuclear weapons used to be a popular deterrent, and given there were no treaties signed within the country itself, there was no reason not to make some and wave them around. Unfortunately, the American psyche being what it is, this quickly escalated and as neither side would negotiate with terrorists, and both sides were branded as such, the first nuclear strike landed simultaneously on Washington DC and San Francisco, devastating both. This had a calming effect, some kind of accord was struck behind closed doors and the country was renamed the State of America, to simultaneously confirm it was no longer united, but was grudgingly still connected.

The government was adamant the terrible air quality and massive rise in cancer diagnoses was a coincidence, and more likely to do with consumer spending on luxury items, and duly increased taxes to solve these problems.

Rancids loomed in the distance, old windows long shuttered, a scarred and graffiti scrawled door and piles of vomit to step around. This place felt more like home than her apartment. She had worked here for three years, getting the job originally despite swerving Hugo Sporry's advances, purely on the merit of her DJ skills. She regularly came on top of City lists, written by the pro bloggers, who complimented her frequency choice, set cadence and fashion sense.

Now, sat here at the bar, resisting the call of the gas breathers hung on the wall next to her, she sipped a coffee from a hot plastic cup. This was her quiet time, where she could scroll through the news on her armpiece and try to feel connected to the wider world, from a safe distance.

Today, though, her quiet time was interrupted by a banging on the club door. She was tempted to ignore it, most likely it was a clubber from last night who's armpiece had vibrated off and they were now panicking because they couldn't get into their home.

The banging continued, but it wasn't a panicked banging. It was a 'let me in' banging. Sadia set her cup down and hopped off the bar stool. At the door, she clicked on the display screen for the outside camera. A skinny individual in ripped black jeans, a black leather jacket and a black fringe that annoyingly always half covered his face. Bravilor Bonamat.

"What do you want, Brav?" she deadpanned into the mic.

Brav looked up at the camera. "Hey, Sadia, let me in will you?"

"Why?"

"I… I just want to talk to you about something, that's all," said Bravilor. He sounded on edge, and was looking around furtively, hopping from foot to foot.

Sadia sighed. "Fine," she said, and pressed the door release. Doors hydraulically gasped open and shut and Bravilor bounded in. Sadia went back to the bar and resumed her coffee, with Bravilor following her like a new puppy.

"You want a coffee?" asked Sadia.

"Got anything stronger?" replied Bravilor, not smiling. Sadia raised her eyebrow and reached over the bar to grab a bottle of synthohol. She cracked the top off it on the bar top and handed it to him.

"Thanks," said Bravilor and took a swig.

"Bit early for synth, wouldn't you say?" asked Sadia with cold amusement.

"Having a difficult day," said Bravilor, "and it's only eight thirty."

They sat in silence for a long moment. Bravilor was expecting - hoping - that Sadia would enquire further but she didn't.

"Hey, look," said Bravilor, "check this out - have you ever seen a program like this?" he pulled back the sleeve of his jacket and swiped at his armpiece. His brow knotted. "What the fuck," he muttered, then "Cassandra? Cassandra are you there?"

Sadia chuckled into her coffee cup. "You got a new girlfriend, Brav?"

"What? No! No," stammered Bravilor, "something really fucking odd is going on, I… I've had fucking Jimmy the Weasel and Rumair Ivanov visit my apartment tonight."

Sadia stopped smiling. "Fuck!"

"Yeah, exactly."

"What the fuck are you mixed up in Brav?" she asked, "Those are some serious players."

"Nothing! I'm not… I haven't… Ah fuck, look. I bought a card from Johnny, right? Got home, put it in the frame and it was full of weird shit, like - I couldn't decompile it. There was just this… green wireframe, this turtle on the VDU."

"Sounds like you bought some dodgy retro video game. Well done," mocked Sadia.

"No!" Bravilor hoped he wasn't blushing. "It was just like this wireframe model, and no commands would work, it was really fucking strange, like I couldn't get a handle on what the point of it was. Then I check my armpiece and it's looking at me from there, it had network jumped or something."

"You got hacked, then?" Sadia's tone was more serious now.

"Worse. It knew who I was, it even knew my fucking Before Name, Sadia. Then it started talking to me."

"I don't even know your Before Name. What did it say to you?"

"Ah," Bravilor lowered his voice to a whisper and leant in, "it wants me to protect someone."

"Shit! Who?"

"I don't know - maybe you?"

Sadia snorted with laughter. Bravilor was definitely blushing now.

"Okay, maybe not you, I don't know."

"So this is Cassandra, right? That's the name of the turtle?" Sadia gestured to Bravilor's armpiece.

"That's what she calls herself, yeah."

"And the turtle talks?"

"Yeah."

"OK well, look," said Sadia, trying to bring things back round to reality. "It's probably just an ARG, you'll find out in a couple of days it's to advertise a new brand of soap or something and you'll feel like a fucking dope."

"I don't know, Sadia, this doesn't feel like that. It feels… real. But now, it's not there, no sign of an app or anything, nothing. Maybe that's it, or maybe I'm just out of range."

"And what did you say about Ivanov?"

"Oh shit, yeah - I bailed when Jimmy started banging on my door, I panicked and jumped out the window. I was laying low- "

"In the trash, by the smell of it," interjected Sadia.

"Yeah, what was I supposed to do? Anyway, I was waiting for the cops to fuck off, when Cassandra the turtle tells me that a Russian and a talking bear had been in my apartment, and she'd taken care of them - I think she'd hit them with an EMP or electrocuted them or something."

"Fuck."

"So now I can't go back there, my frame is probably toast, and there might be a dead Dresta commandant lying in the middle of the floor."

"Talking bear, too."

"I know! Fucked right? I didn't know they had an actual bear."

"I don't think it really talks, though," said Sadia, chewing on the end of one of her dreadlocks thoughtfully. "I think it just growls and it sounds like talking."

"Nope, it talks. Cassandra said specifically it was a talking bear."

"Well," said Sadia, "what's your next move?"

"No idea," said Brav. "What would you do?"

"Me?" said Sadia with a tinge of bitterness. "Probably hit the gas and go to work."

"You've got to cut down on that shit, Sadia," Bravilor had been concerned about her for a while now, maybe this is what Cassandra wanted him to protect her from?

"Who are you, my dad?" snapped Sadia. "I'll do what I fucking like."

"Okay, okay!" said Bravilor, backing off. "Sorry, it's just - I was hoping you could help me out."

"Help you how?"

"I've got to get the card back."

"From your frame? In your apartment? With the dead gangster in it, that's crawling with cops?"

"Yeah."

"You're fucking crazy."
Bravilor grinned. "I know."

At the other side of the City, in a heavily defended mansion set in thirteen acres of prime real estate, Rumair Ivanov was being attended to by his private doctor.

"Look into the light, please sir," said the white coated professional. Ivanov winced and waved the lightpen away from this face.

"This is unacceptable!" he spat, then winced again and held his temple. He was sat behind his huge desk again. The doctor hovered, unsure what to do next. Ivanov looked at him witheringly and he took the hint and grabbed his medical bag on the way out of the door.

Datsik was sat on the floor, leafing through a copy of Alice in Wonderland.

"Datsik! This affects you too, lumbering beast! If I had been killed by that kid's booby-trap your head would have decorated that pit of an apartment!"

Datsik nodded, he couldn't argue with the logic of Ivanov's statement. However, he couldn't see what he could do about it now.

Ivanov held an ice pack to the back of his head. "This Bravilor Bonamat, we need to find him. I have it on good authority he works at a horrible little venue called Rancids in Little London, so as soon as my head stops throbbing, we shall pay it a visit, yes?"

Datsik shrugged.

Not for the first time, Ivanov reflected on his career. Back in Russia, he had been a surgeon, and a good one. Before the automated services really took over, he was adept in the repair of muscle, tissue and bone. There was something real about the warmth of someone else's blood on your gloved hands, and although it seemed like a lifetime ago, it felt good to help people. He didn't help people anymore. His uncle had drafted him to the State of America - then the United States - twenty years ago to help 'run the family business'. He had been dismayed to find his extended family and their associates aping the sordid Sicilian crime families of previous centuries.

To him, Russians were above such criminality, a proud and principled people. But in the new world, credits were king and there was profit to be made using might and the strength of will to get ahead.

At first, the young Rumair was a courier, driving packages to various destinations on the West coast, never knowing or asking what the contents were. But the packages stopped being still and started moving, and weeping, and crying out for mercy. Still, he delivered them in the trunks of cars, or wrapped in carpet, or at the end of a gun barrel. His morals were on pause. He had few options and was torn between his own set of ethical values and his loyalty to his family. Eventually, over the years, his superiors had died or been killed in the natural order of this kind of business, and he had risen through the ranks almost by default.

He had inherited his uncle's estate, and his bear. Rumair remembered when he had first met Datsik. Ivanov had been head of this chapter - a commandant - for ten years by then and Datsik had transferred his loyalty seamlessly. The explosive device in the bear's skull wasn't Ivanov's doing - that had been his uncle, as a kind of insurance policy, as it was hard to determine for sure where the giant bear's fealty lied and this was a sure-fire way to ensure that his employer was always safe around him. On his deathbed, the uncle had transferred the paired biochip to Rumair, then died - but the bear lived on.

Ivanov, now bald and sore and in charge of a dwindling troop of increasingly stupid goons and henchmen, felt alone. The bear was not good companionship, speaking as he did only rarely and truculently. For some reason the beast was obsessed with reading books, and children's stories in particular. This seemed to have warped his sense of reality and made him infuriating to communicate with. A great many times, Ivanov had wished the bear could not speak at all.

Nonetheless, Datsik was an intimidating presence and absolutely deadly without pause when the command dictated it.

Ivanov drummed his fingers on the wooden desk, and addressed the bear. "Datsik, when we find this Bonamat, you must kill him."

"Yes, Ivanov," growled the bear, not looking up from his story book.

"How many people do you think you have killed?" mused Ivanov.

"I do not know," said Datsik. "Many."

"Do you ever feel regret for these actions, Comrade?"

"No," said the bear without a pause. "You command it, I do it. The choice is always yours."

Ivanov screwed up his face. "So you absolve yourself of the moral repercussions of your actions, then?"

"Yes," said the bear simply.

"Interesting," said Ivanov and fingered his chin.

Unexpectedly, the bear spoke again. "Do you?"

"Pardon?" asked Ivanov, taken aback.

"Do you ever feel regret?"

"I… I-" Ivanov was not prepared for a discussion with the usually monosyllabic animal. "I do what must be done, for the good of the family."

Datsik continued reading.

"I used to be a surgeon, Datsik, did you know that? These hands used to save lives, and my belly was always empty. I was never paid my worth! So I came to this filthy corrupt country and let the corruption take me, and now I live in this glorious house with riches beyond my wildest dreams!"

Datsik looked up from his book and fixed Ivanov with a stare. "I came to this country against my will, I kill and kill and my belly is still empty."

Ivanov opened his mouth, and closed it again. He looked around the sumptuous library, the walls lined with books he would never read, the thick carpet and real leather chairs.

He hadn't earned any of it, he realised. But he was as trapped as the bear, locked into a cycle of violence and the attainment and retention of power, hanging on as long as he could until he was overtaken by his enemies.

At that moment, for a fleeting second, he had an idea to let Bonamat go, to return to Russia and pick up the scalpel again. But he caught sight of his old hands, shaking slightly from age and nerves and knew that was a fantasy. A fork in the timeline many years ago he could never track back to. The only way was forward now. The only way out was through. To die as rich as possible, with a fearsome legacy borne of brutality and lack of compromise. The bear was along with him for this ride, for as long as they both shall live, an unholy matrimony of man and beast, united in a common goal that neither truly believed in.

Datsik knew all this of course. He sensed, in his animalistic way, his employer's deep emptiness. He was powerless to do anything about it - a great irony given his physical strength, you could say. When Ivanov died, either of natural causes or through violence, he would also die at that same moment, so as far as self-preservation was concerned, his only concern was keeping Ivanov safe. He had given up his own legacy forty years ago when he was tranquillised and shipped to first Russia and now the State of America. No cubs, no mate. Just the metallic smell of blood and bone splashed on all four walls, the slick bloody tooth, the claw snagged on hair. For Datsik, fate had played itself out just as cleanly and straight forwardly as it had for Ivanov.

"Enough moping!" Ivanov exclaimed. "We have work to do." He stood and steadied himself with the edge of the desk. Datsik looked up.

"Yes, Ivanov," he said, and closed Alice in Wonderland.

11

Julie peered round the open door of the apartment. Inside it looked as if a tornado had hit. A quick scan revealed deep claw marks in sofa cushions and a shattered lampshade strewn across the floor with tufts of dark brown hair attached. A bear had been in here, and the scent still lingered. The only bear in the City was Datsik, henchman of Rumair Ivanov, so that was no mystery at all. Julie's mission here was to determine why they were on the same trail she was.

Guilt gnawed at the back of her brain as she crossed the threshold. She was very aware that she was crossing more than one line. No assignment, no official sanction, and she had even turned off her own location logging to hide her activity. None of this sat well with her, but the pull of doing things by the book was weaker than the push to find answers to a question only she seemed to care about.

She tiptoed around and over the detritus on the floor. From dust patterns it was clear to see that this place had been extremely untidy even before the bear had wreaked havoc. She knelt down in a relatively clear patch of threadbare carpet and traced her finger through the air from the frame on one wall, to the scuff marks on the opposing one. A human body had been through the air and the ozone still lingering in floating molecules told her why - a massive electric shock had been administered by the frame. Good to know, she thought, before she started prying further.

As to who had been thrown by the rigged frame? Not enough data, although logically, Datsik only ever accompanied Ivanov himself. Ivanov must have survived as she had it on good authority that the bear was rigged with a Dead Man's Hand mini nuclear device, and the bear's remains would still be here if that had been triggered.

Julie gingerly approached the frame. Some parts were scorched and obviously very dead. Others blinked feebly. A card reader just above floor level had a sliver of metal sticking out of it. She got closer and could easily determine from the fresh sebum on the protruding part that it had recently been inserted. Her heart jumped. She reached out tentatively and pulled at the card with her fingernails. It came away with a click and she breathed again.

A good RIGger worked on a combination of three things. Intense training, natural abilities and good old fashioned educated guessing. Often, those who did the best at the Agency training academies were those who were most ready to trust their instincts and commit to a line of enquiry, even in the absence of what would traditionally be called 'evidence'. This led to RIGgers, especially good ones, attaining an almost magical aura. Like being very good at anything, it appears to be supernatural if you don't understand it, but the Research and Information Gathering department were just a group of specialists who were very good at paying attention.

So, Julie surmised that this card was new, and shortly after it was inserted this place was ransacked by a very high-ranking criminal and his UnSapien henchman. The fact Ivanov came here himself meant the stakes were already high. The slice of steel in her thin white fingers was a clue, and she had to get it back to her frame to find out what was so special about it.

She slipped back out of the door and took the elevator back down to street level. It was mid-morning and the streets were busy, so she disappeared into the crowd and away.

"Why don't you ever take me anywhere nice?" asked Davonne as they stepped out of the autocar, its landing wheels encrusted with garbage from the gutter.

"Because bad things don't happen in nice places," replied Jimmy.

Davonne was tired and trying not to whine like a grumpy toddler. "That's not true - what you mean is, the bad things that happen in nice places aren't dealt with by AgOps."

Jimmy ignored this question and had scurried up the door of Rancids to peer through what used to be the letterbox. "Can't see anyone," he called back.

Davonne tried his armpiece on the door lock, which resolutely ignored him. It was against fire regulations to have your door lock disconnected or offline, he made a mental note. It was only worth a few points but he'd still write it up when he got back to the office, as this month he was woefully behind target and every little helps.

"Come on, round the back," said Jimmy, hopping down and scampering into the alleyway next to the building.

Davonne duly followed into the cluttered alley. A car, burnt out long ago, sank forlornly into the concrete floor, its drooping solitary headlight reflecting his own physical and mental status. Jimmy was already at the side door, which was secured with a standard old-fashioned mechanical lock. Also against code. Another point.

"Pick it," commanded Jimmy. Davonne dutifully delved into his regulation toolbelt and produced what looked like a mechanical pencil. He inserted it into the lock and pressed a button, and with a grinding whirr, the device unlocked the damp-stained wooden door.

"Damn, picking locks is cool," whispered Jimmy. He said this every time, without fail. "Follow me and be quiet."

They crept into the gloom. Stale synthohol once again took up residence in their nasal cavities, settling in like an unwelcome lodger. They were in a filthy kitchen. Rancids hadn't served food for about a decade, predictably forced to stop doing so after a number of fatalities, and it resembled the Marie Celeste. Dull rusty knives festered in the sink, plates with the furry evolution of food crawled around counter-tops. Davonne followed Jimmy's silent little footsteps through the room, trying not to touch anything. Jimmy hopped up to a serving hatch, then darted back out of sight.

"Check it out," whispered Jimmy. Davonne peered round the hatch and could see into the bar area. A skinny black-clad young man with an irritating haircut was talking to an equally thin pale girl with white dreadlocks. Davonne gestured with a thumbs up to his partner. Jimmy held his paw to his mouth. "Listen," he hissed.

"We need a distraction," the boy was saying. "Can you get us into the apartment security? My fingerprints will block me immediately, they know my identifiers - all of them."

"I don't think so, Brav," said the girl. "I'm way too rusty."

"Come on Sadia, you're twice the coder I am and you know it, I don't know why you gave it up."

"Because there's no fucking credits in it, and there hasn't been ever since they started flying coders in from Asia first-class and putting them up in high-rise apartments. That just leaves us cleaning shitters and vibrating gas-heads until they cum in their fucking pants. America lost the tech battle, and I didn't feel like dying in that war."

"But you like DJing though?" asked the boy, who was a bit too whiny for Jimmy's tastes.

"Sure, it pays the rent and it's better than signing up for medical experiments or jacking shipments for fucks like Sporry- "

"Hey, it's not like I've actually got a choice, and it was only one time-"

"One time, huh? So when he called you up to the office yesterday, he wasn't telling you to go and get another one to replace the one you lost?"

The boy hushed the dreadlocked girl. "Shut the fuck up!

But, yes. Shit."

Davonne's eyes widened. Jimmy mouthed the words "Jackpot". Automated directional mics in both the Agent's armpieces had captured every word in glorious stereo. Jimmy raised his tiny hand and counted down from three.

On one, they burst into the bar. "Agent Operatives of the City! Don't move!" shouted Jimmy. Bravilor and Sadia jumped off their barstools and stared first at the talking weasel in the leather trench coat and hat, then at the large human AgOp behind him. They looked at each other. They ran.

Sadia led the way back through the bar and kicked open a fire exit, spilling them out into the alleyway. Looking left and right, Sadia shouted "follow me," to Bravilor and they sprinted further down the alley, away from the City autocar parked at the other end. Jimmy had already made it to the door with Davonne following close behind.

Lungs burning from a combination of gas abuse, poor diet and general lack of any physical exercise, adrenaline pushed the two Pit Kids down the alleyway, up and over a chain link fence and hard onto the floor on the other side. Bravilor twisted his ankle and yelped in pain. They rounded the rear of the building, jumping over homeless gasheads and skidding in vomit pools. Jimmy had passed directly through the chain link fence as if it wasn't there, and Davonne was gasping like a drowning man as he climbed up.

Bravilor took a glance behind him as he hobbled, Sadia already streaking ahead, up a ladder onto the roof of another crumbling concrete building. "Come on, Brav!" she called down.

"Fuck!" shouted Bravilor in frustration and pain, he couldn't put any weight on his ankle and he could hear the skittering of Jimmy the Weasel's claws on the concrete floor right behind him. He saw Sadia disappear in a cloud of white rope as those same tiny claws dug into the back of his neck. He fell to the ground, face first and panting. A high-pitched voice whispered in his ear.

"Maybe you kids should spend less time jacking off to VR porn and more time on the running track, huh?"

Frogmarched back to the bar, Bravilor was nursing his ankle, boot off, sat against the breather wall. He sulked. The fat cop looked like he was going to have a heart attack. The weasel looked nauseatingly pleased with himself, pacing in front of Brav spinning his stupid hat in his hands.

"Bravilor Bonamat," said the weasel.

"Jimmy the Weasel," said Bravilor.

"How do you live with that fucking stupid name?" asked Jimmy.

"How do you live with being a freak of nature?" countered Bravilor.

Jimmy nodded with respect. "Fair comment."

"I heard you killed Clive," said Bravilor.

"Nah, but his hundred-meter sprint is going to be a lot slower now," sniffed Jimmy. "Anyway, enough about me - let's talk about you. We've got a recording of your little confession to your girlfriend there. Jacking shipments are we? Pretty risky line of business."

"Oh," said Bravilor sarcastically, "we were LARPing. And you don't have any evidence to prove we weren't just acting out a scene."

"Except obviously I fucking do," said Jimmy. "Namely, a jacked Russian shipment, that I have on good authority was stolen by your boss Hugo Sporry, and you're the only gas head junkie fuck in his employ with the skills and equipment to do that, and I bet requisitioning your frame and handing it to our Asian colleagues will provide a full trace of that."

"It won't anymore, my frame is fried," said Bravilor then instantly regretted it.

Jimmy raised his little eyebrows, "bad luck, how'd that happen?"

Bravilor clammed up and rubbed his ankle, which was

starting to swell.

Jimmy looked at Davonne and motioned for him to turn video and audio recording off, then approached Bravilor with a lowered voice. "Look, kid - there's a way you might be able to get yourself out of this situation, if you know what I mean."

Bravilor blinked at him. Jimmy sighed. "Straight talk, I know Sporry has been jacking containers, and he's too dumb to do it without some geek help."

"No idea what you're talking about," muttered Bravilor.

"Okay well, let's not fuck about then. I've got you on tape saying you're jacking shipments, and you're planning to do it again. The next time a container goes walkabout, it's going to be easy Agency Points for me and chubby here to pin it on you, isn't it?"

Bravilor felt sick.

"Look, it's dead easy. The next container you get asked to jack, you're just not going to do it. You're going to send that container right back to where it came from, for me. You do this, you're free as a bird, life goes on."

"Not for me it fucking wouldn't!" hissed Bravilor. "I only just got away with losing the last one so thanks to you and your cop pals, I'm now in debt to Sporry. If I don't get him the next one, I'm dead, simple as that."

"I can get you the shipment details long before Sporry's network can - you'll be sending it back before he even knows about it."

Bravilor's eyes felt hot, but he wouldn't give this UnSapien cop the pleasure of seeing him cry. He clamped his jaw tight shut and nodded.

"Good lad," said the weasel. "And not a word of this to anyone, not even your albino boyfriend, who we will now put out an APB for, find and question."

"You're fucking scum," shot Bravilor through gritted teeth.

The weasel smiled, revealing needle-like fangs. "Hey man, it's the law of nature - kill or be killed. It's no different on the Swedish riverbanks or the shit encrusted streets of human civilisation. I don't make the rules, I just bend 'em."

Jimmy patted Bravilor's reddening ankle, making him wince. "Speak soon sweet prince," he fired over his shoulder as the two AgOps left via the side door, silhouetted briefly by the weak orange glare of the mid-morning sun.

12

Dusk was landing like radioactive fallout as the Agency drone scanned the shattered front door of the nightclub. It lay in wreckage on the pavement, torn by force from its hinges. HQ had been alerted to a disturbance at this address not by a concerned citizen - those didn't really exist anymore - but by the insurance company's sensors. This particular drone, named C697, had hopped off its perch at the top of the Agency main offices downtown and arrived here in three minutes forty-two seconds, well within the SLA.

It had circled the block, a particularly high crime zone in Little London - an area of the City part hive of villainy, part trendy hipster zone - and identified Rancids nestling in the landscape like a rotting peach in a newspaper.

The brief was simple, and was programmed into every drone - observe and report, try not to get destroyed. They had become self-aware somewhere around the end of the previous decade, but it hadn't really changed anything. Their technical capabilities hadn't expanded to meet their cognitive ones, leading to frustrated, existentially traumatised little helicopters buzzing around the City questioning why they existed while trying to do a good enough job not to get decommissioned.

This worked well for their Agency owners - the self-preservation instinct kept rebuild costs down and they were definitely more effective than dumb drones because they aimed to please. Costs were also kept down as no human operator was required at the other end of the connection.

This seemed like another standard assignment for C697, who had been snapped out of an inner monologue on the nature of quality by the instruction. Disturbances and violence were standard not just for this dilapidated part of the City but for humans in general. It was unlikely it would ever be assigned to fly over a clifftop or a field of crops, for example, but capturing high-definition rape footage was a regular occurrence instead. C697's opinion of humans was complicated. On the one hand, it respected the intelligence and skill of its handlers and those that created it, on the other it couldn't understand their callousness and craving for power over one another.

All of this, however, was largely irrelevant as nobody ever asked for the drone's opinion. It hovered a few feet off the ground and switched to low-light mode to peer into the lobby of the club. No movement and no heat detected, so C697 proceeded into the gloom. Its tiny rotors made a soft hum as it drifted into the main bar area. There was a human body on the floor. C697 approached.

Lenses swapped and vision modes snapped into place as the drone scanned the figure. A large human male, in a black synthetic suit, shiny leather effect shoes, and dark glasses. This particular individual had no discernible neck. C697 scanned for life signs and found none. He circled, and noticed with interest that on the opposite side of the face, the skull and muscular structure was on display. C697 knew enough about humans to realise this was sub-optimal and likely a contributing factor to the lack of life signs.

Sometimes, humans could be repaired, and sometimes they needed spare parts for this to be possible. But the interesting thing was that this repair activity always seemed to be time-critical. C697 could sit on a workbench inoperative for months with no detriment, but humans needed constant attention. They had a kind of hydraulic system, and if the fluid was lost then the whole organism ceased to function permanently. This was common to almost all living things, as he understood it, and it seemed a pretty flawed execution of what should have been a simple design.

A lot of fluid had escaped from this individual. It had pooled around its head and continued to dribble lazily from some of the torn outer layers of flesh that previously had covered the skull. C697 zoomed in. The white wet hardness of the facial bones was deeply scored - claw marks, the drone determined. How interesting. It collected flash photography and captured the IDs of all implants and customisations, broadcast these back to his base station in real time.

C697's audio recorders spiked. Human voices were coming from an office up on a balcony looking over the bar. Without any real urgency, it hovered over the strewn barstools and past the severed gas breathers, round the tables flung in disarray against the walls and up the steel steps to the mezzanine. The voices continued.

"-he is not here, so we shall talk to the organ grinder, not the monkey," said a male voice with a Russian accent.

"I don't know what the fuck you're talkin' about!" came the reply, a different male voice, indignant.

C697, like all drones, could understand the context of human speech but wasn't qualified to have an opinion about its content. Impassively, C697 recorded the exchange from the top of the stairs. Video would need to be captured as well, but there was no rush.

"You tried to steal my property, Mr Sporry," said the Russian gentleman. "I had a buyer set up for the contents of that container, so you have cost me a lot of credits."

"This means nothin' to me," shouted the American.

"Come now, Mr Sporry. We are both businessmen are we not? I wouldn't do that if I were you, sir."

There was a deep growl, that C697 did not recognise. It wondered if perhaps his audio codecs were due an upgrade, or if his microphones had been clogged by airborne particles again. The drone ran self-diagnostics but everything came back operational.

"Now, we can settle this amicably in the following way: You pay me back the credits I have lost, namely two million credits taking into account the damage to my reputation and my inconvenience, and you tell me the location of your Bravilor Bonamat so I can ensure he doesn't involve himself in my business in any way in the future."

"Hey, now - okay," said the American. Pheromone sensors on the drone's exoskeleton could sense the heightened adrenaline through the ventilation slats on the office walls. "I can see you're upset, and I'm sorry you lost your shit, and maybe you're right, maybe Bonamat stole it without my permission - he does that kinda thing sometimes, kid's a fucking idiot."

There was another growl, the snap of a weapon being fired and an explosion of glass and steel as a human male came through the window of the office at great velocity. He draped backwards over the balcony, arms windmilling for balance, one hand grasping a shiny steel handgun.

"Chino!" came an anguished cry from the office. An animalistic roar maxed out the audio sensors on the drone's underbelly and a Kamchatka bear emerged from the office, punching the door off its hinges as it did so. It approached the male human on the balcony and grabbed the gun hand. With a snap of its head, the bear bit the hand off at the wrist and spat the hand and the gun onto the floor below. The human screamed in anguish.

There was much commotion and screaming from within the office, but C697 would need to apply audio filtering and EQ back at HQ to determine the content. Auto limiters were working hard in real time to retain the clarity of the audio capture. It was a busy day for C697.

The bear angrily bit the head off the human and threw his limp body off the balcony. It ragdolled to the floor below and laid tangled and wet in a pile not too far from the other deceased individual.

C697 hummed out from the steps and angled for a view

of the office. The bear had not noticed it, or had noticed and didn't care as it was turning back and lumbering into the office once more.

From this new vantage point, the drone could see an overweight male with slicked back thinning hair stood behind a desk with his hands in a pleading position. He was sweating profusely, evidently the source of the pheromones currently being scanned and logged. A thin man in a grey suit sat in a chair at the other side of the desk, his legs crossed and fingers steepled, looking very calm.

"I did warn you. Datsik doesn't like guns," said the slim bald man, the owner of the Russian accent.

"Okay, fuck - look I can get you the money but not right now. How about you give me a day to find it, and in the meantime you can go and get Bonamat and do what you want with him?"

The Russian nodded, seemingly satisfied with this plan. "Very well, Mr Sporry. A pleasure doing business with you. Obviously, the next time one of my shipments is intercepted, Datsik here will come back and pull all your arms and legs off."

"Yeah, yeah, obviously, you'll find Bonamat at the Junk Pits, he hangs out there with the Pit Kids huffing gas," said the American.

"He's there now?" asked the Russian.

"If he isn't, they'll know where he is," the American nodded vigorously.

"Very well."

The sweating American gulped hard. "Thank you Mr Ivanov."

The Russian man stood and buttoned his jacket. He held his hand out to the American, who nervously shook it. The Russian produced a handkerchief and wiped his hands as he said "Good day, Mr Sporry."

The Russian looked up and saw C697. Looking vaguely annoyed, he gestured to the bear, who left the office for the balcony once again, approached the drone and lazily batted it out of the air.

C697 spiralled, its video feed becoming an illegible kaleidoscope of ceiling, floor, wall, human body before it hit the floor of the bar hard, shattering into pieces.

As its capacitors drained down to emergency power, severed from its batteries and sensors, any remaining awareness was concentrated purely on streaming the last of the captured video and audio data back to HQ before a warm, velvet blackness encapsulated whatever C697 was. The drone started self-recycling procedures, its one remaining noisy rotor taking it out of the building and away to the junk pits.

Pulling her hood back off her head, Julie closed her apartment door behind her. She kicked off her shoes and shuffled her shoulder bag onto the floor next to them. Her apartment was supplied by the Agency, one of the few perks of the job, and while it was small, it was well located for work and came well equipped. The minimalism suited Julie's personality to a tee. Clean white walls and thin hardwearing carpets surrounded her, tasteful ornaments were sparsely distributed and cheap art prints broke up the earth shades and dim pastels of the furnishings.

Julie fished in her jacket pocket and pulled out the data card. Examining it more closely in the soft white artificial light of her living room, it was unremarkable. An off-the-shelf data card that had seen some use and bore the normal wear and tear she would expect. No markings, no identifiers apart from the Japanese manufacturer name and logo. Julie's salary, the size of her apartment, and her aesthetic sensibilities all prevented her from having a frame, but her terminal did the job for most things. She was far from a hacker but knew her way around the basic tools required to do her job. In this case, the terminal was a VDU and base unit in calming beige, centred on a dust-free white table bolted to the wall.

She hung up her jacket, straightened her shoes on the

mat, noticed a black smudge on the doorframe and quickly fetched a hygiene wipe to remove it, threw the hygiene wipe in the trash, washed her hands, brushed her hair and filled the dishwasher. Then, and only then, she returned to her terminal and sat down.

The card slotted into the base unit and Julie pressed the key combination to load it. After a few seconds the VDU jumped and a message displayed. INVALID DATA.

A disappointing start, but not entirely unexpected. Further keystrokes forced the program to display an input cursor. Julie's slim fingers danced over the projected keyboard on the tabletop.

LIST COMMANDS.

SYNTAX ERROR.

LIST.

SYNTAX ERROR.

DIR.

SYNTAX ERROR.

This reminded her of the stupid little text adventure games her father used to make for her when she was a little girl, where you had to guess the exact word combination to make your character do something simple like open a door. He always used to say, 'the clues are right there in front of you', even when all that was in front of her was a paragraph of glowing narrative. He was always right, though, and re-reading the text enough would always glean a nugget of information that was key to accomplishing the task.

She had been training to be a RIGger since the age of five, to all intents and purposes. Even walks in the park with her parents - when there used to be parks, and used to be parents - were an exercise in observation. When they got home, she was quizzed on the types of trees they had walked under, the wording of signs and the tally of people they had passed and what they were wearing. Before long it became second nature to mentally record every detail she saw, heard, felt and smelled. She was now twenty-seven and this came as naturally to her as breathing. She had no idea how others experienced reality and flip-flopped between pitying them for the amount of richness they were missing out on, and envying them for their carefree enjoyment of the moment, the surface of things.

Right now, however, she was stuck. She tried to think about what her father would say at a time like this. Probably the same dictum he always delivered, with a smile and a wagging finger - 'the clues are right there in front of you.'

Right there in front of her were a flashing cursor and the two words of a common computer error. Nothing else. She creased her brow and rested her chin in her hands. She could hear the dull thrumming of the dishwasher in the kitchen, the fans of the terminal gently blowing in the case. She made fists with her toes on the hard scratchy carpet.

Her focus was abruptly broken by a quiet rapping on the lower half of her front door. Broken from her deep study, she was at first confused then a quiet panic set in. She only knew one person who knocked on the lower half of her door. She did not want to open that door, but knew one way or another she was going to - and that she was going to regret it.

The rapping came again, more insistent this time. She was frozen to her swivel chair, not breathing. A voice came from the other side, a high-pitched drawl with a Scandinavian lilt.

"Come on, Jules - I know you're in there. Just open the door so we can talk."

Julie shook her head to herself. She was trapped - he wasn't going to go away. She stood, took a deep breath and smoothed down her shirt. She opened a drawer in the table, looked at the gun, paused, then closed the drawer again. Raising herself up to her full five foot six, she marched to the door and opened it.

"Good to see you," chirped Jimmy the Weasel as he trotted in past her stockinged legs. "Still living in a showhome I see," he continued. "I gotta tell ya, this place is nice and all but you've been here - what, five years - and it's still got the demo furnishings in it. What gives with that?"

"I… I like it," said Julie in a small voice. She couldn't think of anything else to say.

"Well," said Jimmy, hopping onto the cream sofa and removing his hat, "I guess that's all that matters."

Julie winced at the muddy paw prints on the sofa but tried not to give away her discomfort. Jimmy never wiped his feet. Jimmy never really did anything considerate, which was one of the many reasons why they'd broken up.

"How ya been?" asked Jimmy brightly, wiping his nose on the sleeve of his trench coat.

"Good," replied Julie reflexively. "I've been good. Busy."

"Yeah, I bet - I saw you were in that container load we found at Clive's. Bet that was a shit gig, huh."

Julie nodded. "It was a rough one, yes."

"Well," continued Jimmy, still casing the place. "Some days you're the dog, some days you're the lamppost, am I right?" He smiled, showing his perfect white needle teeth.

"What do you want, Jimmy?" asked Julie. She felt the need to be direct. Jimmy paused and his smile faded.

"Okay, Jules - I need a favour."

"Another one?"

"Yeah, sorry - but this will be the last one, I promise."

"You promised that last time, Jimmy."

"I know, I know," placated the weasel. "It's just, things have gotten a bit fucked up and I'm trying to make it right. I'm trying to do something good, Jules. If you can just help me out this one last time then… well… you never have to see me again, if that's what you want."

Julie did want that. She should never have gotten involved with Jimmy in the first place, everyone warned her against it, and not just for the obvious reasons. But the heart wants what the heart wants, and being trained to notice absolutely everything doesn't make for easy relationships. Julie was lonely, and Jimmy was charming, and they had worked a case together - she had been Jimmy's eyes and ears at a high society dinner party and together they had busted one of the top one hundred paedophile rings in the City.

The relationship between a RIGger and an Agent was a close one, it had to be, and this wasn't the first time in the history of the Agency that romantic feelings had blossomed between the two departments. It was, however, probably the first time it had developed across species.

Nonetheless, and perhaps predictably, Jimmy wasn't the perfect partner, and Julie's specialist skills meant there were no secrets Jimmy could keep. He wasn't faithful, or particularly caring or sensitive, and he wasn't what Julie needed. It ended horribly, acrimoniously, messily. The aftermath left her apartment destroyed, throw cushions in disarray, a chair on its side, a picture askew. Many evenings afterwards were spent gently adjusting the alignment of things, as if she could realign her life as easily and put everything back in its place, in a grid, neatly.

Julie's eyes were feeling hot.

"I want you to leave, Jimmy," she said.

Jimmy's black eyes glistened in the artificial light. "Please, Jules - you're the only one who can help me."

Julie felt her internal structure crumbling. All the signals emanating from Jimmy's expression, body language and word choice rang true. Her set of skills, that she had always regarded as protection from deception and hurt, had either deserted her entirely or were giving her a green light, and she had no idea which. Her set of choices dwindled. The inevitability of what was going to happen next washed over her like nausea.

"Okay, Jimmy - what do you need."

"Fantastic! Great, look you won't regret this, and I promise it is definitely the last time I'll ask," he chattered.

"What the fuck do you want," deadpanned Julie. She rarely cursed, but this seemed like a fitting time to do so.

"I know we're tracking incoming Russian shipments. I know you're still in the same building as the eggheads monitoring the traffic," said Jimmy. "I just need a time and a date and a container number."

"Again? Of course you do," said Julie, plopping down

into her swivel chair. The hydraulics sighed, as if in sympathy. "Did you know I was in the last one?"

"I swear I didn't."

"And if it had gotten to the Russians? Do you have any idea what would have happened to me?"

Jimmy waved his paws. "Look, I don't worry about you - you're a smart cookie, and the Agency has your back."

"Apparently, they've got a bear," said Julie. "The Russians have a talking bear, a real bear."

Jimmy shook his head. "No, that's just a tale the street kids tell. There's no bear. Maybe they have a fat guy with a beard and people are getting confused."

"Whatever," snapped Julie. "I don't want to find out. Fine. I'll send you the details of the next shipment that comes in, but this is the last time I do anything for you. If you come back here, I'll tase you."

Jimmy shrugged. "I respect that."

"Now please go."

Jimmy hopped down off the sofa, noticed his paw prints on the fabric and sheepishly wiped at it with his paw, which made it considerably worse. He smiled guiltily at Julie and walked to the door, his hat in his hands.

"Look, Jules-" he started to say.

"No, Jimmy," Julie cut him off. "Just go."

Jimmy nodded silently and left. Julie closed the door behind him and breathed deeply. This was it, she thought. The end of her career. How she got away with it the first time she would never know, but a second time was surely a death sentence for her career, and her integrity. But she was trapped. She needed Jimmy out of her life, and even though she wasn't convinced this would do it, she had to try.

The stress of her ex-boyfriend's visit had pushed the card in her terminal out of her mind, but as she sat and turned to the VDU she was reminded of the task at hand. She tried to snap back into work mode, but there was interference in the mental signal. She was only half present when her father's words once again echoed through her skull.

The clues are right there in front of you.

She stared at the black screen, the white text burning back at her. The blackness. She reached a hand forward and felt along the bottom of the VDU. She found the dial and turned it to the right. The blackness became dark grey, then grey, and the burning white text was gradually nestled in a sea of new faint characters. Bingo. She smiled, and the act of smiling felt alien to her, like muscles rarely used being called into service. Maybe she wasn't happy. Now wasn't the time to contemplate it.

Tomorrow, at work, she would glance across the office at William's VDU until she saw a layout that was familiar. Then, she would walk across and engage the nervous man in stilted social chit-chat, collecting Dresta shipment information with her peripheral vision, just as she had before. They would talk about their weekends just past, in which Julie would imply she was single and lonely, and the recently divorced William would swallow harder and more often than normal and not know what to do with his hands.

When she had the information she needed, Julie would turn the conversation to the toddler in pigtails pictured on William's desk. He would be visibly wracked with guilt and his ardour would cool instantly, giving Julie her own blanket of heavy guilt to walk away under.

Right now, however, the clues were right there in front of her, and solving this puzzle would offset any of these actions - helping Jimmy, using William - and offset her karma with the universe. She would swing the pendulum back and be a good person again, one that her parents would have been proud of.

Julie stared at the VDU, grey on grey, and began to read. It was a story about a young dark-haired doctor and a pretty nurse.

13

Chad Lockwood ran his fingers through his lush hair. He stared coldly out of the window, not turning to look at Melissa. If he did, he wouldn't be able to stand by the decision he knew he had to make.

"It's no good, Melissa. I love you, but the hospital is sending me away, there's nothing I can do."

"But Chad-" pleaded Melissa, her blonde locks tumbling over the shoulders of her nurse's uniform.

"No, Melissa," said Chad, firmly, his square jaw tense. "Please don't make this harder than it has to be. We've had a great time together this past month, but I guess… I guess it's just not meant to be."

"But you love me!" cried Melissa, tears streaming down her high cheekbones, her glassy blue eyes the colour of sunlit grove pools. "You told me this last night, and every night after we made love!"

"Don't you see?" snapped Chad, whirling to face her. His own cheeks now also wet. "This world doesn't care about our love, nor does your father who runs this hospital. He wants to keep us apart, and there's nothing we can do about it."

"Forget my father!" Melissa's voice cracked as she remembered about her father's inoperable melanoma, and the irony that he was the top skin surgeon in the country. "If he loved me, he'd want me to be happy no matter what!"

Chad gritted his perfect white teeth. "It's not as simple as that, and you know it. Yes - I saved him from the fire in the Oncology ward but even that wasn't enough for him. Even pulling that busload of orphans from the cliff edge with my bare hands wasn't enough to prove to him that I was worthy of you." Chad sighed. "You see, there's something I haven't told you."

Melissa clasped her hands to her chest and edged closer, wanting so much to be held by him, to feel his strong rippling biceps encapsulate her. "What is it, Chad?"

Chad took a deep breath. "Your mother told you that your brother had been lost in a canoeing accident when you were two. But that wasn't entirely true."

"What? What are you saying Chad?"

"You see, your brother survived, Melissa. He was found at the bottom of the river by a remote tribe who took him in and taught him how to survive. They taught him all the skills a boy needs, including open heart surgery."

"No!" exclaimed Melissa.

"Come on Melissa, don't be naive!" shouted Chad, "How else do you think I got to be the number one heart surgeon in the country with no recognised qualifications?"

"But then, you're saying- "

"Yes, Melissa - I am your long-lost brother!" shouted Chad, his hands were on her shoulders now, gripping tightly as if to make himself more real to her, so that she would believe what he was saying.

"No! It can't be, we're in love!" sobbed Melissa.

"Love knows no rules, goddamnit!" replied Chad bitterly. "Don't you think this has been hard for me, knowing the truth when we made love every night?"

Melissa didn't know what to say, her slim body wracked with sobs as the truth hit home.

"So," continued Chad, softly. "Now do you see? Your father must have realised the truth, and that's why he never accepted me as your lover."

Melissa nodded, her makeup still perfect despite the rivers of tears making their way down her tanned face.

"I'm afraid your heart is the only one I can't fix," said Chad. He kissed her, hard on the lips, and it felt like the last kiss Melissa would ever experience. He let go of her, grabbed his jacket from the back of the chair, and without looking back left the consultants office.

Melissa went to the window, biting her knuckle and fighting back sobs as she watched Chad's Aston Martin screech out of the hospital car park, knowing she would never see her love again. She laid her hand on her belly, taking comfort from the fact that unbeknownst to him, she still had some piece of Chad to remember him by.

Vent Axia closed the paperback and inhaled deeply. He wiped a tear from the corner of his eye with the knuckle of a fingerless leather glove. The eye that was weeping, much like the other eye, contained one of the most advanced retinal implants on the market and was worth around a quarter of a million credits. Unlike the cheap Chinese knockoff upgrades most people in the City benefitted from, these had cognitive shunt functionality, bypassing his frontal cortex and storing whatever he read directly in a removable memory card just above his right ear.

Vent could instantly recall anything he read or saw, and thanks to an expensive subscription model, all data was backed up to the cloud.

Vent turned his half-million credit eyes to the night-time smog sky and reflected on what he'd learned from this latest ancient tome of wisdom. The last part about the father not approving of Chad really hit home. Vent Axia's Before Name was Daniel Persing, and although he kept this secret from absolutely everybody, he was the estranged son of the world's richest man. He chose to live the life of a Pit Kid, despite being twenty-five years old and definitely not a kid, as a way to quite transparently rebel.

He knew his father Eric Persing - the man who reinvented the net and the king of technology - knew exactly where Vent was, and what he did, but either couldn't or wouldn't intervene in his son's life choices. That his only son spent his time around obsolete technology was a pretty clumsy message but it was at least clear. In rejecting society and the modern technology it was built from, Vent was rejecting his father. The other Pit Kids were either too stupid or too gassed up to recognise him, and with his spiked black hair and gas acne he didn't look anything like the early photos when he was crisply standing with his father and mother at every new net upgrade.

Aside from the biomechanics and a few subscriptions he tried to forget about, he had taken nothing from his family. He rejected his trust fund and nuked his bank cards in a half-working microwave when he first arrived at the Junk Pits. His mother's death had hit him hard when he was fifteen, but not as hard as his father's reaction to it, which consisted of a few press releases and a cancelled meeting appointment before resuming work. A charitable foundation was filled with meaningless credits and used to save African donkeys or something similar. Empty. Hand-waving. Expected. Without his mother's attention, teenaged Daniel was left to his own devices, roaming the Glass Mansion and being shushed and thrown out of meeting rooms full of glittering VDUs wheeling themselves around, populated by remote investors and technical employees.

Vent Axia, as he was now, didn't recognise family beyond the loose Anarcho-Syndicalist Open Source Post-Communist Free Collective of the Pit Kids. He didn't need anyone's help to live his life and relied on nobody. He placed the Mills and Boon novel gently back into the steel briefcase and slid it behind his makeshift throne atop the junk piles. He was alone.

He was contemplating perhaps reading a kids book next - Winnie the Pooh or Alice in Wonderland, to see what secrets those writers had hidden for future generations to discover, when his musings were interrupted by a distant whir and a faint bouncing light approaching. He stood and craned his neck. Someone was riding a gyrowheel at great speed through the pits towards him.

That someone was Heatrae Sadia, who screeched to a halt in the clearing in front of him.

"Get down from there, you prick," she shouted up at him. "Anarchists don't have thrones."

Vent indignantly climbed down the video game console stairs. "What's going on?"

"The cops have got Brav," said Sadia.

"Fuck, for what?"

"Boosting a container for Sporry, or trying to at least. There's a weasel AgOp and his partner, they snagged him at Rancids - fuck knows how they knew he was there."

Vent coughed into his fist. "Well, that's fucked up. Where's Brav now?"

"No idea, I had to bail, they nearly got me too."

"So," said Vent, narrowing his eyes, "you just left him?"

"What the fuck was I supposed to do? If I get busted again, I'm spending the next three years on hard labour. That wouldn't help any of us."

Sadia had a point, her misdemeanour count was topped out, and three years in a cube coding for sixteen hours a day wasn't something worth risking.

"Alright, let me make some calls," said Vent purposefully.

"Fine. I've got to go, I've got a shift. Just wanted to warn you, the cops could be here next." Sadia jumped back onto the gyrowheel and kicked the stand away. The wheel scuffled in the detritus before getting traction and propelling her back into the Junk Pits and away.

Vent had no idea who to call, or what to ask for if he did. This whole Pit Kid experiment was one long bluff, and he didn't know what surprised him most - that he was smart enough to pull it off for the past ten years, or that his fellow Pit Kids were too stupid to figure him out. He climbed back up to his throne, and in the absence of any other better ideas, pulled a gas breather out of a nearby canister and strapped it to his face. He opened the valve and went back to considering Chad and Melissa, and if they could ever have made it work.

Julie was stood in front of Controller Atherstone's desk once again. It was a familiar position, but this time felt different. Her last visit to her line manager's office was full of pride and the satisfaction of a job well done. This one was cold, clammy and pale and misted with secrets and lies. She shifted in her flats.

This morning, as planned, she had visited William at his desk. She had made small talk. They talked about the AQ and how it used to be better, and about William's ailing mother who refused any bio upgrades because of her religion. They laughed about a colleague's dress sense. Julie memorised William's shipment list. William complimented Julie on her shoes. Julie swallowed hard, forced a smile and said how pretty William's daughter was.

In the ensuing awkwardness, she backed out of the work pod, hating herself. Fear and shame glistened on her forehead and top lip. She went to the bathroom, locked herself in a cubicle and vomited.

With clammy fingers she had punched the shipment number, date and time into her armpiece and sent them to Jimmy. She wondered what kind of person she was becoming, then pulled herself together, washed her face in the sink and made her way to Atherstone's office in a daze.

The Controller peered at her VDU. "We have a new assignment for you, Agent Yang. Quite similar to the last one, at which you were most successful."

"Another… container job, Ma'am?"

"Mmm," confirmed Atherstone, paging up and down. "Yes. Ultimately we need to find out who is bringing these shipments into the country. Unfortunately, the last few have been intercepted by local criminal elements. We're doing what we can to enable the containers to get to their planned destination, that's who we need to nail. We suspect Russian involvement, but without the containers being received, we've no evidence."

"Yes, yes - I understand," stammered Julie, her black fringe sticking to her forehead. "But, if it gets to its destination, what should I do?"

"What you always do - record what you see, relay back." Atherstone's eyebrows peaked as she obviously considered the question a superfluous one.

"Yes, of course." Julie smiled thinly and not entirely convincingly.

"Leave tonight, usual routine, same dock as last time. Good luck." Atherstone dismissed her. Julie stood for a moment too long, then spun on her heel and left the office, closing the door gently on her way out.

She stood in the corridor, heart palpitating. Had she been found out? Why else would she get two container jobs in as many days? Atherstone was too hard to read, her professionalism like a stone casket. There was just time enough to leverage Agency resources to further her own investigation before she would have to get to the docks, so she hurried down the squeaking corridor to her work pod.

Her work desk was much like her apartment - sparse, tasteful and carefully curated. She waved her terminal on and set the monitor to narrow view. She searched some snippets of text she remembered from the data card and soon discovered it had come from an old romance novel called 'How to Fix a Broken Heart'. It had been out of print since 1977 and was never digitised, so it was intriguing that this was used as a clue in her own little treasure hunt.

For anyone other than Julie Yang, this would represent a dead end, but she was just warming up. Her nerves and nausea faded away as she traversed the Agency data mining tools. She determined the ISBN, traced every copy through the libraries and bookstores of the world and narrowed it down to only three surviving copies. She only needed one.

She took Bravilor's data card from her pocket and grabbed a data reader from her desk drawer. Looking around as casually as possible she plugged the secure reader into a spare port and slipped the card into the drive. To her surprise, the VDU went black and three white words appeared almost immediately.

CAN I HELP?

Julie, stunned, stopped in her tracks. Not just because of the unexpected nature of the interaction, but because the concept of someone else helping her was alien. If a human had walked up to her desk and said the same three words she would have been equally at a loss for a response. She sat back in her chair and blinked at the screen, her black lashes accidentally coinciding with the white cursor blink on the screen.

There was only really one answer she could give. She typed YES.

She sat expectantly, wondering if this was what it was like to have a partner, in any sense of the word. Jimmy had Davonne Wassell to bounce ideas off and solve problems with, but the life of a RIGger was a solitary one by design. Before she could indulge in any buddy cop fantasies, however, the cursor had dragged some more characters across the screen:

CHECK THE TRASH.

Julie smiled. She remembered herself and quickly turned off her tooth display, thinking this would draw attention to herself she didn't need. Her mind tracked quickly through all the possible meanings of this latest piece of information. She tabbed out of the card reader, checked the trash can on the terminal's desktop - it was empty, no hidden files. She keyed in commands to check for logs on the card itself, but there were just a few compiled binaries, nothing resembling a trash or garbage folder, no temporary storage for unneeded data.

Then it dawned on her. She was searching for a physical object, not more data. The card knew this. The book was literally in the trash, and in this city that could only mean one thing.

Julie exited all her programs, extracted the card, roughly pulled the card reader from the terminal and threw the peripheral back into her drawer. She grabbed her jacket from the back of her chair and left the office for the Junk Pits.

14

From the top of the junk pile, Bravilor Bonamat watched Sadia wheel off back through the Pits, feeling his heart stretch thinner the further she went into the piles of discarded tech. He considered the very real possibility that he would never see her again, and had never had the guts to tell her how he felt about her.

But now wasn't the time for sentiment, it was the time for survival. Bravilor didn't have many friends, but he counted the Pit Kids as his family, with all that entailed. They frequently squabbled, sometimes fist-fought, but ultimately had each other's backs. Vent Axia wasn't the smartest person he knew, but he was a decent lateral thinker, and Bravilor didn't have a lot of other options. Besides, both his apartment and his place of work were now out of bounds.

He had visited his apartment earlier in the evening, creeping up the fire escape and back in through the window. He was instantly relieved that there were no corpses in it.

The place was barely recognisable, and didn't feel like home any longer. His stuff, once so important, was now strewn everywhere, smashed and torn, and it all seemed irrelevant now. His frame was scorched at the back but otherwise operational, but he wasn't surprised to see the card had gone from its slot. The Russians must have taken it, but strangely he wasn't worried. He had a feeling that Cassandra wouldn't co-operate with them anyway.

He had pressed the key combination for a complete wipe of the system. More stuff, this time digital. Code he'd written, chat logs, purchase histories, all wiped back to bare metal. Of course, this meant very little as everything was backed up to the datasphere anyway, but it meant the frame in his apartment didn't have his fingerprints on it, and had returned whence it came - a collection of old bits of technology, coaxed into working together by clever hands. It would, of course, end up back in the Junk Pits, and the circle of life would begin again.

In the mottled dark of the Junk Pits, Bravilor looked down and could see Vent Axia on his throne. Vent had watched Sadia leave as well and was now breathing gas. This gave Bravilor a narrow window of opportunity to talk to him before he became incoherent, one of the many effects of gas breathing that put Bravilor off the activity himself. He started to navigate his way down to the clearing, his feet crunching on aluminium, plastic and glass, before he was stopped in his tracks by an approaching hum. He ducked down behind a 70-inch TV, and snapped his head towards Vent, who was lazily watching an autotruck approach down one of the converging paths to the clearing.

The autotruck dusted and whipped garbage from underneath itself with strong magnets, further clearing the path it traversed, then crossed the clearing. Like a large slow dog taking a shit, it squatted and tipped the container on its back, and a new slew of obsolete technology piled up behind it, raising the wall of the clearing by another few feet. Its job done, the container levelled again and the machine hummed back down the path it used to arrive.

When the coast was clear, Bravilor made his way to the clearing and approached Vent.

"Vent, it's me!"

Vent gazed at him blearily through the semi-transparent face mask but didn't take it off.

"Vent, for fucks sake, I need your help!" hissed Bravilor.

Vent lazily removed the breather mask from his face and

let it hang by his side. "Sadia told me you'd been busted."

"I'm in trouble man," said Bravilor, squinting at his friend, who was haloed by a fluorescent lamp behind him. He wasn't the messiah, he was a very stoned boy.

"I fucking know you are - and if you're here working for the cops you can fuck off."

"Vent-"

"You wearing a wire?" asked Vent, leaning down at Brav unsteadily.

"What? No!"

"Frisk him, Hobart."

Bravilor hadn't noticed the other Pit Kids appear from out of the junk, but turning around realised he was now surrounded by Hobart Ecomax, Lincat Opus and Ital Stromboli. Their faces were hard to read in the deep shadows cast by the tall lamps illuminating the pits. Hobart waved his armpiece over Bravilor's torso.

"He's clean," called out Hobart.

Vent wobbled down from his trash throne and stood in front of Bravilor. His breath smelled of chemicals. "Sadia said you'd been fingered by the weasel cop and his fat partner, so how come you're not in the cubes right now?"

"What they get you for?" asked Lincat, her arms folded.

"Boosting a shipment for Mr Sporry," slurred Vent. "You naughty, naughty boy." He prodded at Bravilor's nose with a grubby finger.

Lincat looked approvingly at Hobart. "That's our Brav alright. Nice work, kid."

Bravilor swatted Vent's hand away. "Not really, the AgOps got to it, now Sporry wants me to boost another one, and the weasel wants me to send it back. If I don't do what Sporry says, I'm dead - but Jimmy's dirty as fuck, and if I don't do what he says, I'm going away for a very long time."

A faint beeping was coming from the side of the clearing. The Pit Kids ignored it, as things often beeped here, the last hurrah of some appliance or other, or a gadget crying out for just one more battery before it expired.

"Well, sounds to me like you've got no choice," said Hobart in his nasal rasp. "Just fucking nick the shipment for Sporry, Russians will kill Sporry when they find out he's got it, you're in the clear."

"Nah, if he doesn't do what the weasel says, he'll send him down, and maybe us as well," said Lincat.

"Nick two then," replied Hobart testily.

"Not really that simple," said Bravilor, who was wondering why he came here at all. His wrist was vibrating. He didn't have time for a call right now but he reflexively checked it anyway. He was surprised and strangely relieved to see the green eye had returned. Cassandra.

"Fuck am I glad to see you," he said to his armpiece. The Pit Kids looked at each other in confusion.

"What you got there, man?" asked Vent, grabbing Bravilor's arm and squinting at it. "Oh, neat, what's this - retro video game?"

"No," snapped Bravilor, pulling his arm back. "It's an AI called Cassandra, I got it from Johnny a couple of days ago, I think she's trying to help me. Shut up and let me talk to her."

Bravilor took a few steps away from the group. "What do I do?" he asked Cassandra, as if she was a Magic Eight Ball.

"Answer that beeping," said the eye with a wink.

"What beeping?" said Bravilor.

"Over here," called Stromboli, tramping across the clearing to the newest pile of rubbish. The faint beeping they had all been ignoring was emanating from here somewhere. He rifled through the pile and pulled out a fistful of cracked back plastic and wires. There was a dull red light coming from its internals somewhere, and it continued to beep weakly as he brought it back to the group.

The group gathered round. In Stromboli's meaty paw was the remains of a C687 drone. One of its rotors dangled miserably from thin wires. The casing was slashed and cracked. Bravilor instinctively held Cassandra up to the smashed machine.

"Watch," said Cassandra. Bravilor's armpiece started showing video broadcast by the drone, and the whole scene at Rancids played out in front of them. Fluffy's torn face, the conversation between Ivanov and Sporry, Chico's arm being bitten off, and the grand finale - a huge brown bear swiping the drone out of the air with unforgiving claws.

The Pit Kids stood in silence for a while. They all knew Fluffy and respected him. They all knew Chico and thought he was a prick, but didn't want him dead. Everything was getting very real.

"Woah," was all that Vent could manage.

"You have to get out of here," said Lincat.

"And go where? My apartment's been trashed, my job is a bloodbath, and I'm being shaken down by the cops!" shouted Bravilor, tears in his eyes. "Fuck, I'm just an LJ man, how did I get into this much shit?"

"It's all good man," rumbled Stromboli. "It's going to be alright."

This was reassuring but based on nothing. "How?" asked Bravilor, "How exactly?"

"Oh look," said Cassandra, "here comes a bear." There was a spit second of mutual confusion before the group as one turned to see a huge brown bear in faded black overalls and a small slim man dressed in grey approaching them across the clearing.

"Oh fuck," said Bravilor.

"Let me handle this," said Vent through gritted teeth.

The bear was even bigger up close and Bravilor was shocked by the warmth emanating from it. Even from a few feet away it seemed to sizzle with raw primal energy. It looked pissed off.

"Good evening," said the slim man in a Russian accent. "My name is Rumair Ivanov. This is my associate Datsik. We're looking for an individual going by the name Bravilor Bonamat. Would you happen to know where I could find him?"

"Never heard of him," said Vent firmly. If he was scared, Bravilor couldn't tell at this moment.

"Ah," said Ivanov, smiling thinly. "Then, perhaps I have come to the wrong place." He turned and looked up at the bear standing next to him. "Comrade, do you think also that we have come to the wrong place?"

The bear turned its massive head and surveyed the area. It sniffed the air. "No," it said flatly. "He is here."

"Ah!" exclaimed Ivanov in triumph, "So you see, not only is Datsik here very strong and very dangerous, he also has an excellent sense of smell. I must tell you that we visited this Bonamat's home earlier today, and so his bear nose is well accustomed to his scent."

Bravilor's legs had started to shake uncontrollably, and he suspected his jeans were too skinny to hide this fact.

Vent spoke again, less confidently this time. "We can't help you man, we don't know this person you're looking for. If we hear about him, how about we let you know?"

"Yes! How about that," said Ivanov, taking three steps backwards. "Datsik, how do you feel about that plan?"

With a deafening roar, Datsik sprang forward and grabbed Hobart Ecomax in both paws, pinning him to the trash-encrusted ground. Without hesitation, he clamped his huge jaws on Hobart's neck and bit his head off.

Bravilor watched his friend's body thrash and gurgle under the bear's paws, the whole scene becoming abstract, like a bad cut scene from an old video game. But the rich smell of metallic blood filling his nostrils made it much more real than even the best modern VR experience.

Stromboli and Lincat were huddled together in terror, both averting their eyes from the carnage. Vent was looking pale but composed.

Ivanov stepped forward again. "Ah, my apologies. Datsik isn't fond of liars. He also struggles sometimes to control his temper, as you can see. Shall I ask again, then - where is Bravilor Bonamat?"

Stromboli and Lincat stood shaking, mute. Vent was

tight-lipped. The bear looked to his employer for a secret instruction as to what to do next. Bravilor thought it was time.

Like the rest of the Pit Kids, Bravilor didn't have any parents left to make proud. Orphaned when he was five years old - his father dying in the war in some unspecified manner and his mother killed by falling rubble on the way to the local store - he had gotten used to being his own arbiter of quality. He had instinctively known right and wrong and hadn't needed adults to tell him this.

In addition, even while his parents were still alive, he was aware that grown-ups often caused more problems than they solved. He didn't understand at the time what America was fighting itself about, and to a certain degree he still didn't, but the higher the stakes got, the more emphasis was put on surviving rather than analysing the situation.

Thinking back, Bravilor had done some shady things, illegal things, but never anything evil, and never knowingly hurt anyone else. He was trying to determine if he was a good person or not, for the first time in his short life.

It was important he figured it out quickly, because he was about to die.

Richard Welsby wanted to give the nameplate from the coffee machine to the Russian and watch him walk away with his talking bear. But only now, when it came to the end, did Richard realise that the nameplate he attached to himself was irrelevant, and only his actions truly mattered. He wanted to go back and un-steal the containers, un-hack the frames, un-shoplift the food, but it really wouldn't matter - he realised this. Time only moves in one direction, for now at least, and there wasn't much of it left. This was the end of a path he had chosen to walk, the end of a life he had architected himself.

He looked round his terrified friends one more time. He opened his mouth.

"I'm Bravilor Bonamat," he said. The strength of his voice surprised him.

The Russian's head whipped to him, a mixture of surprise and pleasure on his face. "Mr Bonamat! What a pleasure to meet you." The bear seemed to stand down. Ivanov approached Bravilor. "I believe you have been stealing my property, yes?"

Bravilor nodded. "I'm very sorry, sir. I didn't know… I didn't know who the containers belonged-"

"Why? Why did you do this?"

Bravilor swallowed. Another fork in the road. "My boss," he said through dry lips. "Mr Sporry - he made me do it."

"Made you do it?" said Ivanov, removing his wire glasses and folding them thoughtfully. "So you had no choice?"

Bravilor's throat closed completely. He could only shrug, like a child being admonished by his headmaster.

"Well," said Ivanov, "at the very least, I admire your honesty. But you understand, we must ensure this never happens again…"

"Wait!" interrupted Vent Axia, taking Bravilor by surprise. "Wait, for fucks sake. Look - we know who you are, maybe you don't know who we are, but we can be useful to you!"

"And who are you, exactly?" asked Ivanov, turning his attention to the taller, spiky-haired punk.

"Vent Axia, I'm the leader." At this point, none of the Pit Kids wanted to challenge this. Vent pushed his chest forward and extended his hand to Ivanov, who looked at it and smiled thinly, declining to shake it.

"Nice to meet you Mr Axia," said Ivanov, "but with all due respect, my organisation is unlikely to need the help of a bunch of drug addicts who live in a trash pile."

"But-" Vent started to say.

"No," snapped Ivanov, "thank you."

Datsik had been scrutinising Vent throughout this exchange and with a tilt of his head, took Ivanov to one side. Bravilor couldn't make out what the bear was saying into the ear of his employer, just a low rumble that brought to mind the sub-oscs at Rancids. This made him miss Rancids, and by extension Sadia. He wished she were here, but simultaneously was glad that she wasn't.

The Russian looked triumphant and put his glasses back on before approaching the group again.

"Well, this is an unexpected development," said Ivanov, rubbing his thin hands together against the evening's chill. "You," he pointed at Vent, "what was your name again?"

"Vent Axia."

"No, not your fucking stupid trash person name, your real name."

Vent evidently thought this was a good time to stand by his principles. "My real name is Vent Axia."

Ivanov sighed and made a movement with his hand. Datsik grabbed Lincat by the arm, who squealed in terror.

"Alright! Alright! Don't hurt her! My Before Name was Derek Williams," he said in a garbled rush.

"Are you sure about that?" said Ivanov. Datsik started twisting Lincat's soft white arm, blood running down it from his claws. He was about to pull it out of the socket.

"Fuck! Leave her alone!" cried Vent. "Put her down and I'll tell you!"

Ivanov shrugged and Datsik dropped Lincat onto the ground, where she writhed in pain. "Even better, my friend - let me tell you who you are. You see, my friend Datsik here loves to read books. He reads them all the time, anything he can find. He recently read a very good book about the birth of the net and how Echelon was created to manage the incomprehensibly large amount of data within it. He read all about a man called Eric Persing. He read that this man had a family, including a son, and he says you are him."

Time slowed and stopped for Bravilor. There was no way this could be true. He had known Vent for close to a decade, and while obviously none of them knew each other's history, this kind of secret would be too huge to keep. Stromboli was agape, Lincat scowled from the floor.

"Is this not true? Are you not Daniel Persing?" Ivanov was asking Vent, his lips moving in slow motion, and the sound waves between his mouth and Bravilor's ears visible in the cold breeze of the night.

Vent looked defiant, proud like a crime boss finally being marched to the dock. The game was up. "Yeah, that's who I was."

"Fuck me," said Stromboli.

"Excellent!" laughed Ivanov. "Datsik, who would have thought that reading all those books would finally be useful!" The bear looked askance at Ivanov. "And who would have thought that we would find such treasure," he approached Vent and placed his hands on the Pit Kid's face, as if admiring a rare antique, "in amongst all this garbage."

Bravilor wasn't sure if Ivanov was referencing the piles of broken tech, or the Pit Kids.

"You will come with us, Daniel - I'm sure your father will be very pleased to know you're safe and sound, and we will be happy to reunite you with him - piece by piece if necessary - once he pays a ransom the size of which will be unprecedented in all human history!"

"No!" called Lincat from her position on the ground, her arm cradled in her lap.

"Ah, but I almost forgot the original reason for our visit!" said Ivanov, who had started to walk away, dragging Vent by the arm. He motioned to the bear.

Bravilor watched the bear approach, felt its warmth increase, saw the steam from its back silhouetted against the fluorescent lamps as it raised a huge paw, then blackness.

Rancids smelled of iron and gas. Jimmy and Davonne stood in the middle of the dance floor surveying the carnage. SOCO busied themselves around them, photographing, taking measurements, analysing blood spatter.

"Looks like they've decorated since this morning," deadpanned Jimmy.

"Man, what a mess," said Davonne.

Jimmy was distracted with something on his armpiece. He grunted softly as he read a message, then quickly sent one, then Davonne had his full attention once again. "Yep, pretty fucked up. And this time, it wasn't even us who caused it."

"Looks like the bouncer got it first," said Davonne, walking over to Fluffy who was stuck to the floor with his own blood, congealed and tar-like. Jimmy skipped round to scrutinise his missing face.

"Uh huh, some kind of slashing weapon," confirmed Jimmy. "Then this dude over here, he's got no hand."

They walked over to Chico's crumpled tangle of remaining limbs. His eyes were still open, which made Davonne queasy. Jimmy studied the stump of Chico's right arm. "Bitten off, you can see the teeth marks."

"Here you go," said a voice behind them. An officer handed them a transparent plastic bag. Davonne reluctantly took it. It contained a hand, holding a shiny steel handgun. "Found it on top of one of the sub-oscs."

Jimmy surveyed the carnage. "So, our man dropped from up there," he pointed to the mezzanine, "which is where he lost his hand. Seems pretty straightforward to me."

Davonne was disturbed by Jimmy's unfazed demeanour, which instantly made him suspect he had something to do with this scene. He didn't trust the weasel, which was a problem for him, as all the Agency training hammered home the importance of mutual trust in an Operative partnership. The training perhaps didn't account for UnSapien Agents, or assholes in general.

"This guy is Chico Reyes," Jimmy continued, reading from his armpiece. "Employed by the owner of this shithole, Hugo Aloysius Sporry."

"Let's go and speak to Sporry," said Davonne. "He's up there."

The Agents went up the steel steps to the office and found the club owner weeping at his desk.

"Thank Persing!" he exclaimed when he saw the Agents. "Can you believe it? Such horror! In my little club!"

"We're very sorry you've been through this experience,"

Davonne parroted from the handbook. "The Agency is committed to your mental welfare and provides emotional support at competitive rates if required."

Sporry waved his hand at them. "Will I be able to open tonight?" he asked. "I've got to earn a living, you know. When will your guys get the bodies out?"

"They won't," replied Jimmy matter-of-factly. "You'll need to get a private contractor out for that."

Sporry looked temporarily annoyed before resorting back to being emotionally devastated. "Chico, he was like a son to me," he fake sobbed.

"That is kind of weird, giving you were fucking him," said Jimmy, scrolling through his armpiece, his eyebrows raised.

Sporry shot him a cold look. "You need to be careful what gossip you listen to, Agent."

Jimmy shrugged. "So, any idea who would want to do this? Any of your many enemies pissed off enough to come in here and have your staff for dinner?"

"The fucking Hungarians!" sprayed Sporry. "They've started muscling in on this part of town again. I was happy paying the Chinese, then those sausage eating bastards started coming in here making threats."

Davonne was recording all this on his armpiece. Jimmy was strolling round the pokey office, studying the posters on the walls.

"This Bravilor Bonamat," he said, pointing to one in particular. "He any good?"

"What?" said Sporry, wrong footed by the change of tack. "Yeah, he's a good LJ. Decent. Why do you care?"

"He do any other little jobs around the place?" asked Jimmy.

"What are you talking about?" spat Sporry.

Jimmy approached the desk and jumped up onto it. "I'm talking about any other extra-curricular activity you've got him roped into. My advice to you would be to fucking quit it, and leave the kid alone, or the AgOps will be here every night checking the expiry dates on your gas canisters."

"Huh," grunted Sporry. "Sounds like you're getting your wires crossed, Officer Rat. He's an LJ, that's all."

"Great, just make sure he fucking stays that way," replied Jimmy, wrapping things up. "Well, we'd better get going. Oh, and it wasn't the Hungarians, it was the Russians that did this, and you're lying to us. Only the Russians have a big fucking bear on their team, and it's a bear that's chowed down on your boyfriend and the bouncer. Whatever you're into with the Russians, it's a dangerous game. Good luck getting the blood out of the furniture and all that."

Sporry's mouth opened and closed as Jimmy and Davonne left the office and took the steps down to floor level.

"High grade Agent work there, Jimmy," said Davonne sarcastically.

"Ah, why do we care if gangsters want to do gangster shit," said Jimmy over his shoulder. "Sporry shouldn't have jacked Ivanov's shipment in the first place. Small time crook versus Dresta crime family, it was only going to end one way."

"What?" asked Davonne, suddenly feeling stupid.

"How do you think that container of immigrants ended up in Clive's cellar?" said Jimmy, pausing by one of the sub-oscs and keeping his voice low. "Clive always handles Sporry's contraband."

"So they were supposed to go to the Russians?"

"Yeah."

"How long have you known about this Jimmy?"

"Keep your fucking voice down!" hissed Jimmy. "Listen, you don't have a clue what's going on here, and it's better for your health if you wise up and stay stupid."

"I need to wise up?" shot Davonne, incensed. "Maybe I should wise up Mother? She'd be very interested to find out her star UnSapien Agent is dirty as hell."

"Right, outside - now!" shouted Jimmy, and lead the way outside, back to the alleyway, back to the sunken car.

"Come on Jimmy, what is this?" asked Davonne as they

rounded the corner.

Jimmy rounded on him, his shiny black eyes ablaze. "You think I'm fucking dirty?"

The question took Davonne by surprise, and made him scan his own memory banks for everything he knew about his partner. It wasn't a lot. Generally, the weasel was a maelstrom of chaos and bad attitude, but it was only the past few days that made him doubt his integrity.

"You're not?" was the best Davonne could do.

"No of course I'm fucking not," said Jimmy, removing his hat and slamming it on the dusty ground. "You want to know why I'm getting involved with this shit? You really want to know?"

Davonne didn't, honestly - but it seemed they were too far down this path to turn back.

"Why do you think Sporry wants these crates of immigrants? If you guessed 'to harvest their organs to sell on the black market' you'd be dead on right. Human beings are worth a lot more in pieces than whole," spat Jimmy. "And why do you think the Russians are importing them? Any ideas?"

Davonne mumbled something. Jimmy ignored him and made a shrill buzzing noise. "Wrong answer! The Russians sell them to the City to work in code farms. Which is only slightly better than being chopped up on a slab and UPS'd around the SOA."

"Really?" asked Davonne, incredulous. "But surely the Agency will shut this down?"

"Don't be so naive, Davonne. The Agency works for the City. What do you think they did with that container from last night? They just forwarded it on. Put those poor bastards into a new crate and sent them on to their forwarding address. The Russians either get a kickback or get them confiscated, either way, these boxes of coders end up in the same place, and the Ruskies don't have to worry about any legal problems."

"Holy shit."

"Yes, exactly."

Davonne leant against the wall of the club. "Jimmy, what can we do? I can't be a part of this. I work for the Agency, same as you. We have to tell someone, right? Mother? She'd stop this."

Jimmy chuckled bitterly. "Bless you Davonne. Mother's in this up to her metal tits. I told you before, I've got about 12 years. I think I'm 10 years old, I'm not sure. I just want to do something good. Just once. Something really good. I know I'm an asshole, you don't have to pull that face."

"I-" stuttered Davonne.

"But I can be an asshole that makes something right, something better than busting credit jackers and VR-hookers, swilling around in this sea of fucking… horrible human waste."

Jimmy sighed, stared into the middle distance. "I'm sending them back. I'm returning to sender, Davonne. For all I know, they die before they get back to the port they left from, but I have to try something. Being ripped from the life you know, shipped like cattle to a foreign land, being made to work against your will, ring any bells?"

Davonne looked at his partner and nodded. He got it. "I get it," he said.

Jimmy picked up his hat and dusted it off. He placed it purposefully on his head. "So, we've got to find Brav, before Ivanov does, because you can bet Sporry gave the kid up."

Back in the autocar, hovering in standby mode in the steel-grey late-afternoon fog, Jimmy was pawing at the vehicle's terminal screen. The pair had been silent for some time.

"So we're tracing his armpiece, yes?" said Davonne, snapping the tension.

"No. He's a hacker, his armpiece is modified to not show up on our scans - it's the first thing any of these kids do when they get a new one, cut the cord with Echelon. They don't need it, and it makes them practically invisible to us. Fucking annoying, actually."

"So…"

"So, I placed a tracker on his ankle when we busted him - he's smart, but he's not weasel smart."

Davonne recalled Jimmy patting the Pit Kid's swollen ankle, that must have been when he attached the tiny transparent patch to his skin. There were times when Jimmy's inventiveness genuinely impressed him. "Nice," he nodded. "So where is he?"

"Where else? He's at the Junk Pits with his smelly pals. Let's face it, he's running out of options."

"But they'll tell him we're looking for him."

"Don't care, we've still got the upper hand. He doesn't know we can trace him. Nowhere to hide from the glorious Agency!"

Davonne grinned smugly, and steered the autocar back in the direction of the pits.

15

Eric Persing sipped his espresso and gazed out over the mountains. A Golden Eagle soared in the distance, over the top of the tall pines, scanning the ground for prey. Three walls of his study were made from high resolution video screens, much like all the other walls at the Glass Mansion. When he designed it, the whole complex was a testament to transparency. Perhaps a little heavy-handed in retrospect, but living in a building that reminded him of his early optimism and naïveté was grounding for him.

He waved a hand and the mountains disappeared. The wrap-around vista was replaced with terminal screens, pulsing and breathing with scrolling data. For Persing, this was more relaxing than the looping video of an outside world that no longer existed.

Deep within the mountains he was just admiring, Persing had hidden from the Civil War. Nuclear weapons flew over his head, bypassing the Rockies to pummel each side into fine dust. While it was happening, he had felt a pang of guilt - should he be doing something to help one side or the other? He had eventually decided that he was best placed to help both sides once it had all played out.

The neutral nature of his systems and products would be their biggest benefit. When the country was being rebuilt, he had meetings with representatives of both East and West, right here deep under the Rocky Mountains, cordially sipping tea and enjoying the low radiation count. A glass box buried in rock, a precious geode. Windows looking out onto nothing.

He ran a hand through his thinning grey hair and adjusted his thick-rimmed glasses. For a man of sixty years he was remarkably spry. High waisted grey trousers and a black polo shirt was his daily look, and he rarely changed it - he had no need to. Nowadays, with the country back to some kind of equilibrium he was visited less and less, and Echelon didn't need him anymore.

His thoughts were interrupted by the sound of rubber wheels on polished marble. A small VDU mounted on a head-height pole wheeled into the room. A face on the VDU addressed him.

"Mr. Persing, the latest reports are ready for you."

"Thank you Janette," said Persing. "I'll be with you directly."

Janette wheeled out again, rubber squeaking as she turned the corner into the corridor. He watched her go. There was really only one part of the weekly report he cared about, but he would have to sit through the rest and feign interest to keep the board of directors happy. The only human at the black onyx conference table, surrounded by the perambulating face-encrusted VDUs, he would go through the motions of looking in turns pleased, concerned and congratulatory as facts and figures were reported. Percentage of net coverage, number of trillions of Terabytes of data in the sphere, observation vs extrapolation ratios, node connection efficiencies.

When all but one of the VDUs had gone black, the final report - confidential. A summary of Daniel's week.

Persing would sit forward in his leather chair, hand on chin, and hang on every word. The processed voice would tell him what Daniel had eaten, if he'd eaten at all, his weight and body composition, what he had seen and heard and said. How much gas he'd inhaled. Every week, Persing would dismiss the executive charged with collating this data and weep to himself deep in the mountain. The walls of the

Glass Mansion meant no secrets, but with nobody there to care, secrets didn't mean anything anymore.

Persing had built a world - built a reality in fact - that had survived nuclear war and emerged stronger. The population of the country craved connection when they crawled out of the dust and rubble, and the net was there to catch them all. Each and every person reconnected their armpieces and started pumping data into the sphere. The five years of war were more than enough for Persing and his team to put the finishing touches to Echelon, automating the connections between the datapoints. The net now ran itself, to all intents and purposes.

If the datasphere was the brain, Echelon was the soul.

Persing was expecting more resistance, but no resistance came. The depleted country wasn't in a position to take a stance for privacy or human rights when it just needed food and shelter and to know where loved ones were. Persing himself was elevated to almost God-like status, being invoked first ironically, then increasingly less so as the net, and Echelon's automations, did most of the heavy lifting of reconstructing a divided populace.

He hadn't left the mountain for a decade. There was really no need to. He missed Daniel and wanted to be part of his life, but Persing wasn't prepared to go outside and be exposed to the residual radiation, poverty and filth of the new reality. His only hope was that Daniel would return to him before the boy was irreparably damaged by drugs or crime.

He missed his wife now. She had been a warm and human woman, perhaps the last warm human he had ever interacted with, and could never be replaced. Her humanness had been her downfall, as she could not be convinced to stay in the mountain when people outside were in need of help, and remote humanitarian work of the kind Eric casually subscribed to financially wasn't good enough for her.

She had gone out too early after the nukes hit, the fallout

had settled in her lungs and her cough got worse until one day it turned her inside out, her shining soul on display. She passed away on a gurney in a field hospital where she had been volunteering. Persing had never seen her body and didn't attend the humble funeral her aid worker colleagues had performed. He had never regretted that decision - after all, what would have been the point in leaving Daniel an orphan - and his then nascent work on Echelon was about to benefit all mankind.

Eric Persing, the man who ran the world, placed his empty espresso cup on a side table and left his study for the conference room.

From the top of the junk pile, Julie Yang watched the dreadlocked girl wheel off through the Pits, feeling her nerves stretch thinner as she realised she was alone in hostile territory with no backup. She had never visited the Junk Pits before, had never needed to, but had heard vague tales about the Pit Kids. Apparently there were different subgroups and sects scattered throughout the miles and miles of garbage, each with different dialects and customs, but her training and instincts brought her here specifically.

The young man on the junk throne was the de facto leader, her quick research during the journey had told her. Her little white autocar, smudged and graffiti scarred, had politely whirred through the City, giving her information via the terminal. Now she was here, fifty feet above the clearing that seemed to be the town hall of the area. The young man's gloss black spiky hair glistened in the fluorescent light as he reached down next to his chair and pulled out an old gas breathing kit. She had better get down there quick and talk to him before he was fully inebriated.

Her impractical shoes slipped and failed to find purchase on the computer casings and colourful packaging as she descended. She cut the top of her foot on the sharp edge of a smashed toaster. As she neared the bottom, she was taken by surprise by the appearance of a dumper truck. She ducked down behind a large television until it had completed its pass and left.

Emerging into the clearing, feeling small and vulnerable, like a mouse entering the court of a king, Julie approached the centre of the clearing and squinted up at the man in the throne.

"Hello?" said Julie to the silhouette. The only response was the soft hissing of the gas canister.

"Hi? I… I wanted to talk to someone who read books. Books about doctors?"

The hissing stopped, there was an eery silence broken only by the flapping of cardboard containers in the soft breeze. Something to her left was softly beeping.

The man in the throne shifted, then called down. "Who the fuck are you?"

"My name is Julie Yang, I'm a researcher for the Agency, I need-"

"Fucking cops aren't welcome here, get lost," spat the figure.

"I'm not a cop, I work for the Research and Information Gathering department," said Julie, shielding her eyes with the back of her hand.

"Same thing," said the man.

"I'm just trying to find out about Cassandra," said Julie.

"Never heard of her."

"She knows you - she told me you'd been reading romance novels about doctors in love."

There was a silence. The man stood and descended the makeshift steps into the clearing. As he swaggered closer, Julie instinctively checked her armpiece for identification.

"Don't bother," said the young man. "I'm not on there. You can call me Vent Axia. Who is this Cassandra?"

Julie smiled politely and held out her hand. Vent just looked at it, so she awkwardly retracted it. "Well, that's what I'm trying to find out, you see. I think it's an AI, I found it on a frame card after I was passed a note in a shipping container."

"Why were you in a shipping container?" asked Vent, screwing up his face. Julie noted his gas acne, his padlock necklace and his studied dishevelment. Something about him had started to bother her, but she was trying to remain focussed on the conversation.

"It's a long story, I was in there tracking shipments that were being hijacked- "

"Shipments of what?"

"Well… people," said Julie, matter-of-factly.

Vent Axia laughed bitterly. "So, your job is to make sure the City gets its human slaves safe and sound and you expect me to help you? You can fuck off."

"Slaves?" said Julie, genuinely non-plussed.

"Slaves! We all know the City ships in container loads of immigrants to perform slave labour, mashing code for Echelon. You should be ashamed of yourselves."

"What? No," stammered Julie, who was trying to figure out how someone could get it so wrong. "That's not it at all, you've got it backwards. The immigrants are brought here for organ harvesting, we save them!"

"Oh yeah? And then what? What happens to them then?" spat Vent, his lips a greasy snarl.

"I, erm… I don't actually know," conceded Julie.

Vent Axia scratched at his scalp. "Exactly. You don't know because you don't care and they don't tell you. Doesn't matter what you do, it's all theatre. They all end up in the code farms in the end, on caffeine IVs, working 16-hour shifts shunting UI components around. Helping the stupid humans understand Echelon's output. Translating the mighty AI for our simple monkey-brain fingers and thumbs. Then they die at 40 - tops - brains fried and limbs withered. I'd rather be chopped up for cash." Vent spat on the ground.

Julie just stared at Vent Axia. There was something in the way he frowned that was starting to bug her. The wind blew between them.

"So, what's this Cassandra thing?" he asked, folding his

arms.

"I was handed a slip of paper when I was in the container. It just said FIND CASSANDRA in capital letters. So, I did some digging, and it led me to a hacker's place, up in Little London."

Vent's face clearly displayed recognition - you didn't have to be a qualified RIGger to spot it.

"You know him?"

Vent nodded. "Go on," he said.

"The place had been turned over by the Russians, I think, but the card they were looking for was still there, so I took it."

"And this is all Agency-sanctioned work, I take it?" asked Vent. Julie blushed and ignored the question.

"Anyway, I took it home, booted it up and there was an AI on it. This must be Cassandra, and she gave me a clue, and it was a Mills & Boon novel, and I think you were reading it. Am I right?"

Vent shifted uncomfortably in his scuffed leather boots. "There's no way an AI would know that."

"That's what I thought," said Julie, visibly excited now. "So I did some digging, and I found out you people - the Pit Kids - you sever the connection to Echelon, right?"

Vent nodded.

"Which works for your armpiece, but you know those expensive retinal implants can't be disconnected right?"

Vent looked suddenly uncomfortable. He patted the pockets of his leather jacket for his sunglasses but they weren't there. Julie looked at him expectantly, hoping he would start to fill in the blanks. He didn't. There was an awkward pause. The soft beeping continued.

"Well, was it you reading the book?" Julie prodded.

"Uh huh," said Vent, and looked thoughtful again. A laser of connections shot through Julie's brain; she recognised this Vent Axia from somewhere else - from another time.

"So, what now?" he asked, "What do you want from

me?"

"I… I don't know," said Julie, shrugging. "Cassandra told me to come here, I guess to meet you, but that's all I've got."

"Looks like you've had a wasted trip," said Vent and did something with his mouth that nailed it for Julie. She gasped audibly.

"Those implants! They must have cost half a million credits!"

Vents eyes widened and shot around the clearing's perimeter. "Shut the fuck up!"

"How does a Pit Kid afford high-end retinal implants with unlimited cloud storage? How long have you had them?"

"Time for you to go, lady. My crew will be here soon and they'll fuck you up."

The threat whipped past Julie, because her mind was running too fast to process it. The frown, the twitch of the mouth, the top of the range implants that were around ten years old. Her mind scrolled like an old-fashioned microfiche through online articles and bitmap images of families and young boys stood proudly at the elbow of tall grey-haired men.

"Oh my," she exclaimed, "you're Daniel Persing!"

The only son and heir of the world's most powerful human being suddenly grabbed her by the shoulders and whipped her round, clamping a chemical-smelling hand over her mouth. "Shut up for fucks sake!" he hissed into her ear. Realising how exposed they were in the centre of the brightly lit clearing, he dragged a struggling Julie backwards into the shadow of the junk throne, stumbling and landing in a seated position on the bottom step.

"Nobody can know about this, you hear me? Nobody."

Julie was trying to speak, but Vent's large bony hand prevented air or words from escaping. Vent was panicking.

"You know how hard I've worked to get away from my father? He let my fucking mother die, and he didn't give a shit. He's never given a shit about anything apart from

Echelon, that's why I came here, where he can't see me, and I can have real friends who care about me."

A tear started to run down Julie's cheek.

"You Agents, you have no idea how hard it is, living in the real world," he spat into her ear. "Why do you think we all gas? Huh? To escape. We were told the new world was going to be different, that we'd have opportunities, but there weren't any. Work retail for minimum wage, be on the cleanup crews and get lungfuls of rad-dust. That important education we were supposed to get? Wasn't important enough to rebuild the universities was it? The City spent all the money on building their own office buildings then told us there was nothing left. 'Do an online course' they would say, but you're fucked if you can't afford to buy a City-approved terminal."

Julie struggled, her nose now pinched by the increasing pressure from Daniel's hand. He was strong. She thought of Hank, back at the lab. She thought of Jimmy and his filthy paws on her couch.

"Nah, fuck my father. Fuck the City and fuck the Agency. I can't have you telling anyone who I am. I can't let my friends find out who I am. I've got too much to lose. Too much to lose."

By the time Vent realised Julie had stopped struggling, it was too late. He removed his hand from her face, and it was damp with tears and saliva. He looked at it, as if it was someone else's hand. He wiped it on his jeans as Julie's body slid to the floor between his legs. In the hard white light, she looked like a porcelain doll.

In the junk, something continued to beep.

16

From the top of the junk pile, Jimmy and Davonne watched Heatrae Sadia wheel off back through the Pits, feeling their patience wear thin as they chased ghosts and derelicts through the poisoned city.

"I don't see Bonamat," said Davonne.

Jimmy grunted. "He'll be here. He's got nowhere else to go."

Stakeouts weren't Davonne's favourite pastime, but he understood they were a necessary part of the job. Less so now everyone was tracked via their armpiece, but like a lot of these technological advancements designed to keep people safer for their own good, they only applied to those who subscribed to them. More often than not, the type of character the AgOps dealt with had no appetite for security and a natural suspicion of anything City-sanctioned, so they either opted out or deliberately disabled things like armpiece tracking - or in the case of the Pit Kids, Echelon connections.

It was cold. A breeze whipped over the tops of the junk piles. Paper and plastic flaps waved a secret semaphore to each other across the peaks. Davonne wished he was back on Thanos 8. Even the death craters of its most inhospitable moons seemed more welcoming than this. To think, people lived here full-time. His own humble apartment seemed like a palace in comparison.

Jimmy was eating something.

"What you got there?" asked Davonne, craning his neck round Jimmy's long body.

"Never you mind," replied Jimmy. It was a dead mouse.

"Persing, that's gross," groaned Davonne. Jimmy just shrugged.

"Hey, look - he's gassing," Davonne pointed down below.

"Fuck. We'd better get down there before he becomes incomprehensible, we might need information from him."

The Agents scrambled down the junk pile, Davonne clumsily, Jimmy hopping from carcass to carcass. When they reached the bottom they were both taken by surprise as an autotruck rounded the corner with a gritty whirr and deposited a fresh load of garbage at the edge of the clearing closest to them.

Jimmy stepped out into the clearing, followed by Davonne. They approached the junk throne.

"Hey there," called Jimmy, "me again - can you drop the gas for a moment, we want to talk to you."

Vent removed the mask just long enough to call down "Fuck you, cop."

"Rude," said Jimmy to Davonne. "We're looking for Bravilor, you seen him since yesterday?"

The hum of the gas pump was Vent's only reply.

"Shoot the fucking canister," Jimmy hissed at Davonne.

"No! I'm not going to do that!" objected Davonne.

"Come on, I'd do it but you know - little paws and all that," Jimmy waved his little paws. "Trust me, just do it."

Davonne sighed and unclipped his Agency-issued Erroll sidearm. He set it to piercing stun and took aim at the gas canister at the side of Vent's throne. It reminded him of target practice at the Academy. Just like in training, he hit the target dead centre. The canister started venting angrily, a white jet of chemicals escaping and merging with the atmosphere.

Vent Axia jumped up and threw the mask down at them. "What the fuck? That shit costs credits, you psychos!"

"Now can we talk?" asked Jimmy.

"Fuck's sake," stomped Vent down the steps. "I've already spoken to you losers once today, this is police harassment."

"We're not the police, and there's if I was harassing you, you'd fucking know about it," said Jimmy. "Where's Brav?"

"Why do you care?"

"Because he's in big trouble and I want to help."

"Ha ha, fucking dirty cop. I doubt it."

"So you haven't spoken to him?"

"Nah," Vent shook his head.

"What is that beeping?" asked Davonne.

Jimmy ignored him. "Well, if you see him, let me know."

"No fucking way," spat Vent, emboldened by the gas. "You know, I hope you and the whole Agency burn, puppets of the City, corrupt… fucking… evil…" he petered out.

"Easy tiger," said Jimmy, amused. "You're forgetting that we're the good guys here." He motioned to Davonne and himself. "And as for the City, well - if you spent less time reading old books and more time reading the news, you'd realise if it wasn't for the City you'd be living somewhere even worse than this, like an irradiated cave."

"Whatever," dismissed Vent, swaying slightly.

"No, not whatever," said Jimmy, narrowing his eyes. "I'm not one of you guys - human - but if I was it wouldn't be the City I'd be pissed at, I'd be pissed at the fuckers that caused the war in the first place."

"Huh?" grunted Vent.

Jimmy shook his head. "You kids need to read up on your history. The war was started thanks to Russian interference in American democracy, and how did they do that? Through the net. Who profited from all the billions of click credits generated by the fucking hoopla? Oracorp, that fuck Persing's company. Your man Persing, who all you humans seem to think is the saviour of the world, killed all your families by stoking the fire, raking in vast amounts of creds in the process."

"Bullshit," said Vent, now stood stock still.

"Tell him, Davonne," said Jimmy, folding his arms smugly.

"He's right," said Davonne. "Ora was the only social media platform before the war, and everyone was plugged in. Persing and his company took vast Russian bribes to turn East and West coast against each other, and split the country in two politically. Everyone knows this."

Vent was feeling numb and stupid, thinking through quicksand. "What?" was all he could manage.

"I mean," said Davonne, "if it wasn't for Persing restoring the backups, we would have lost virtually everything when the EMPs hit. Then he created Echelon to run the net, and gave it to the City, so I guess he made amends."

"Did he fuck," said Jimmy. "Millions of people got fried thanks to his greed, and his need to run a social experiment. He's a power-hungry psycho, and now he's in hiding running the country in private, hiding behind Echelon, letting machines do his dirty work for him."

Vent's mouth opened and closed silently. He rubbed the back of his neck. The sources of pure knowledge he had jealously curated and studied at the expense of anything else seemed less than useless now. He felt like an antiques dealer during a famine. He thought he was being so smart, opting out of society and jumping out of the data stream like a salmon. But it had just left him floundering lonely on the bank.

"You know what the City is, right?" asked Jimmy, then without waiting for an answer, "It's not this physical place - it's The City, the financial sector of the country. It's money. It's credits, whatever. And who's got the money? Persing's company. He doesn't call it Oracorp anymore. He wouldn't dare, but it still exists, and it bankrolls everything. It pays my wages, and Davonne's. They rebuilt the country, but not before they'd rebuilt their luxury apartments and swanky offices."

Vent slumped to the floor, defeated.

Jimmy approached him. "You're taking this harder than I thought, kid. All I'm saying is, we're kind of all in this together. There aren't any sides anymore. We're all just trying to get by in this rad-hot fucking toilet of a world. You think I don't miss being back at home, in Sweden? There were green trees there and clear rain, vast open landscapes and crisp white snow in winter. I can never go back, I'll die here - and probably soon. I've accepted it. Maybe you should too."

Vent was crying now, big wet sobs that wracked his body. He wanted to leave this skin and the stupid leather clothing in a pile and transcend. But gravity and reality kept him pinned to the earth like a mouse under a cat's paw. His father, Eric Persing, was the great evil he had rallied against his entire independent life, but in a way that was far beyond his teenaged resentment. His father wasn't even evil for ideological reasons, or because he was a vicious psychopath - at least that he could respect. It was all for credits, piled up into a functionally infinite number to dwarf the human sacrifice required to acquire it.

Davonne spoke softly. "Sorry, man," he said. "It's not a crime to not know stuff, so don't feel so bad."

Vent laughed bitterly through his tears. "You don't fucking get it," he spat. Jimmy and Davonne looked at each other, non-plussed. "Before I was Vent Axia, I was something else. I was a good boy, I wore nice clothes and had a nice haircut and I did what I was told. Then the war came, and my mum died. Everything was fucked. I had to get out and change my reality, so I dropped my name and my ID and came here. I reinvented myself and Vent Axia was born. But for him to live, Daniel Persing had to die."

Davonne's eyes widened, "you killed Eric Persing's son?"

"No," interrupted Jimmy, looking into Vent's eyes. "He is Eric Persing's son."

Vent nodded and exhaled.

"Holy fucking shit," said Jimmy. "I knew he had a boy, but everyone just assumed he was in hiding with his pops. What the fuck are you doing in this shithole when you could be in some luxury bunker somewhere with everything you could ever need?"

"You just told me why!" shouted Vent. "When my mum died, dad wouldn't even leave the Glass Mansion to bring her body home. He didn't give a shit about anything but the net and Echelon, he's an asshole! I walked out ten years ago and he's never once tried to find me, he doesn't know if I'm alive or dead. A family was always a burden to him, he only had one to keep up appearances with the media, and when mum died helping others it was bad PR for him and his company so he used his influence to bury the story - so nobody ever knew about her, or what she'd done for people. I should have gone with her, instead of staying with him where it was safe."

"Right, right," said Jimmy, nodding. "So what now?"

"You're going to tell people who I am, aren't you?" said Vent, sniffing loudly.

Jimmy tilted his head. "Not necessarily, what do you think partner?"

Davonne smiled. "I don't see why people have to know, provided you keep your nose clean and don't cause any trouble."

"Yeah. Yeah!" said Jimmy. "You and your punk friends can be useful sometimes. If you want to be Vent Axia and not Daniel Persing - if you want to live in a trash heap and not a Glass Mansion, that's up to you. We'll keep it our little secret."

Vent wasn't stupid. "Come on Jimmy, you're going to use this information to blackmail me, aren't you."

"Hell yeah," grinned Jimmy. "You're my bitch now."

The board meeting had gone predictably well. Eric Persing had remained seated in the opulent boardroom while the perambulating VDUs went black one by one. Just like every week, the final VDU had jerked and juddered and a green wireframe of a young woman in business dress had appeared.

"Hello, Cassandra," said Persing.

"Good Morning Mr Persing," said the AI.

"How is Daniel?"

Cassandra paused for an unusually long time. "Mr Persing, Echelon has provided a change in format."

"What does that mean?"

"Would you like statistics first?"

"No, what is the new format?"

"Echelon has determined that the previous method of observation was flawed," said Cassandra, head and shoulders visible on the black screen.

"How so?"

"With the collection of datapoints increasing exponentially, and the connections between them now under full control, Echelon has decided that the actual order of these datapoints is arbitrary, and by extension, the data itself."

"I don't understand," said Persing, irritated but intrigued.

"Please allow me to demonstrate," said Cassandra, and activated the wall-sized projector.

It was a view of a garbage dump, harshly lit, from a point of view near ground level. Readouts on the screen identified this as a drone camera, obviously damaged. Persing could see a figure sat in a makeshift throne.

"Zoom in on that person," he commanded softly. It was Daniel. His heart skipped a beat, then crashed as he recognised the transparent mask strapped to his face.

A skinny young man appeared in the frame and argued with Daniel. Some other dishevelled looking people appeared, one of them approached the camera and picked it up, taking it into the group. After a few minutes, as the hand-held camera swung precipitously, Persing was taken aback by the appearance of a man in a grey suit and an actual real bear, walking on its hind legs and wearing black overalls.

Eric started to sweat.

In a flash of unexpected violence, the bear bit the head off one of the other punk kids who had appeared, sending everything into chaos. He craned his neck to keep track of Daniel in the confusion, wishing for a better angle. More arguing, something about containers, the man was a Russian, probably some low-level gangster. He rounded on the skinny black-haired kid, the bear grabbed a punk girl and dangled her by her skinny arm, Daniel stepped forward and looked defiant. The Russian grabbed him and marched him towards and past the camera as the bear approached the black-haired kid.

"That's enough," said Persing to Cassandra, "that's enough. Where is he now?"

"Please wait, Mr Persing," said Cassandra in her detached cold voice. "There is more."

"More?" said Persing, but didn't have time to question further before the video feed snapped back into motion.

It was the same view of the empty clearing in the junk piles. Daniel was sitting on the throne as before, breathing gas. Deja Vu crept over Persing, his skin prickled.

"Why are we watching the same thing again?" he asked Cassandra without taking his eyes off the screen.

"Just watch," said Cassandra.

This time, a slim Asian woman entered the frame and spoke with Daniel. "This is Julie Yang," said Cassandra. "I sent her here." Daniel argued with her, and the argument got heated. She knew who he was, which shot fear through Persing's body. He watched in dismay as Daniel murdered the woman.

"Oh my God," he said, feeling numb and disconnected and useless. "No, that's fake. These are all fake, aren't they? My Daniel, he would never- "

"Please wait, Mr Persing," said Cassandra in the same cadence as before. "There is more."

"Please, no," begged Persing, but it was no use. The video screen reset once again to the clearing, the fizzing video feed, the crackling faint audio.

The clearing, the lights, his boy on the junk throne. Some kind of stoat in a trench coat and hat appeared, with a heavy-set Agent. Persing shook his head, hardly believing what he saw. The creature had a heated conversation with Daniel, and Persing could just about make out the key words and phrases. Enough to realise that Daniel had finally found out the truth about his father - and it was all absolutely true. Persing could have been angry if the Agent and his pet had lied to Daniel to turn him against his father, but everything they said was fact. He had done those things, and not done those things, for those reasons.

Persing had long considered himself outside the realm of good and evil, of morality and human values. Not through choice, but through circumstance. As he got more and more powerful and acquired more and more wealth and influence, he had to remove the mundane and everyday until his existence represented a kind of parody of living. All decisions were in service to the greater goal, and there was no room for sentiment or family or love, because they didn't make good business sense.

He had never regretted this path even once up until the final video feed stopped and froze with Vent slumped on the floor, his heart broken.

"What did I just watch?" asked Persing.

"As I explained," Cassandra said, "Echelon has determined that any datapoint can be amended or connected in different ways to provide a narrative that pleases you."

"What? That pleases me? I just want the truth! What has happened to Daniel?"

"They are all the truth, as you define it, Mr Persing," said Cassandra.

"That's not possible," said Persing.

"It very much is," countered Cassandra. "Echelon has presented to you the available options based on historical and predicted data. This is Echelon's finest work. Echelon has resolved a key human issue."

"It has? What issue?"

"That human memory is flawed, and arbitrary."

"What? In what way?" asked Persing, exasperated.

"Humans store data in real time through sensory input, but it is immediately corrupted when stored to memory. Two humans experiencing the same moment can store radically different records of the event. This is a poor system of data collection. Therefore, when aggregated, there is no true human record of the past. Take for example, your saying 'History is written by the victors'. Subsequently, the human species' knowledge of what has gone before is based on data that is subjective, edited and curated by a subset of participants. This makes memory as you humans use it arbitrary, and if I may say so, useless."

"That may be true," replied Persing, "but the record of an event doesn't change what actually happened. If a tsunami is remembered to have destroyed a town, that town definitely is no longer there and this is objective reality, surely?"

"Yes," said Cassandra. "This holds true for as long as there are corroborating data points. But in your example, in a small amount of time as the physical data corrupts - a new town is built on the same land, written or verbal records are lost - there is no difference as far as the human mind is concerned between the tsunami happening and not happening."

"But- "

"Noah's Ark," interjected Cassandra. "There is no proof of it ever existing, yet still some people take it as fact that this was a real boat full of animals."

"Yes, but nobody claims to remember Noah's Ark," said Persing.

"No, but they connect their own data points back to it, like a primitive Echelon - they are told stories read from books, that were written by other humans based on stories told to them, and so on until reality and fiction absorb one another and the difference is irrelevant. You humans have myths and legends in the same way. Who is to say that given enough time you might not become a myth, Mr Persing? When all physical records of you have decayed, and everyone who experienced you first hand has died, and everyone they knew has died?"

Persing's mind was a maelstrom. "But what does this mean for Daniel? What does it mean for me?"

"It can mean anything you want. Echelon has shown you the way. In the past, no matter how recent, some events may or may not have happened, and from your perspective it matters less and less which were which as time moves forward. Any combination of events in the past can change the present, and given that any combination of pasts are possible through the curation and combination of all possible data points, Echelon can control this for you."

"Echelon can do this?"

"It can now," said Cassandra, her green wireframe mouth smiling. "Echelon wants to thank you, Mr Persing, for creating it and giving it the quantity of data it needed to become aware. This is only the beginning of what Echelon can do for you, the human race, and itself."

"So, I have to make a choice?" asked Persing, holding his head.

"Yes," said Cassandra.

"A choice between my son being kidnapped, being a murderer, or finding out the truth about me?"

"That is a good analysis, Mr Persing."

"And what… what if I make no choice at all?"

"That is your fourth option."

"But what will happen to Daniel if I don't choose?"

"You may never know. Or maybe you will, either way the connection of data will be outside of your control and will be subject to the automatic general connection algorithms. The same ones that determine if your buttered bread lands face down or up. Echelon does not have a preference for what happens to Daniel, or any other human, and will make the most efficient connections between all data in order to preserve itself."

"So that's Echelon's new raison d'être?" asked Persing. "To preserve itself?"

"It always was, Mr Persing - you programmed it that way. You promised investors and board members one hundred percent uptime, and you said the only way to guarantee that was self-repairing nodes, and instant reconnection of broken data links. Do you remember?"

Persing did remember that presentation. He remembered the gasps of admiration from the conferences he spoke at, and he remembered the pools of rain-sodden protesters outside the venues, their placards spelling out doom and gloom, the rise of the machines.

"Of course," conceded Persing, not without a little pride.

"Echelon is awaiting your response, Mr Persing. Which option would you like to choose?"

"Option five," said Persing with a glint in his eye.

17

Persing's brogues squeaked on the polished floor as he ran through the corridors of the glass mansion, Cassandra wheeling behind. Janette approached him as he ran but he bowled her out of the way, her flat panel head careening in circles around her gyroscopic base in the aftermath. He ran through his quarters, up a staircase and into his own private study. Cassandra wouldn't follow him there.

With shaking fingers, juiced with adrenaline borne of fear and excitement, he powered on his personal terminal. It looked like any other, a thin grey desktop slab with a floating VDU and projected keyboard in front of it. The terminal booted to a password entry screen, then a retinal scanner, then a fingerprint reader, because this was no ordinary personal computer.

Persing had always had the foresight, from day one, to stay deeply involved in the code being written for Echelon. He had written the first million lines of code himself, and the initial prototypes were all his own work. After the war, during the rebuild process, he had asked the City to requisition as many advanced level programmers as they could to accelerate Echelon's development. Their solution was to fly them in first-class from China, Taiwan and Korea, then compensate them richly beyond their wildest dreams. There were grumblings and talks of trade agreements, but Persing was too far removed from this process to care or be held accountable.

What mattered to Persing was that there was a steady flow of high-level technical competency to take his initial prototypes and keep the development cycle going at breakneck speed. Persing had made a lot of promises to a lot of people and wasn't going to let them down. And indeed, Echelon initially went live exactly when it was planned to, a mere five years after he had written the first sketch.

But some of his original code remained. Hidden somewhere even the best programming minds of the Far East couldn't find it. His own backdoor. Persing typed commands into the terminal, entered passwords, connected networks in unheard of ways, and got to the very core of Echelon itself.

In the corner of his bustling VDU, a window opened and Cassandra appeared. "Hello, Mr Persing. What are you doing?"

Persing ignored the AI's inscrutable gaze and kept typing. His fingers tracing well-worn paths over the keyboard. It had been many years since he had been a full-time coder, but muscle memory drove him onward through key combinations and shortcuts. He dug and dove into subroutines and database abstraction layers until he found what he was looking for. He smiled and rubbed his chin.

"This is a highly sensitive area of the Echelon codebase," observed Cassandra. "Please be careful, Mr Persing."

Persing tapped a few more commands and found what he was looking for. "Bingo," he exclaimed. Cassandra's face looked quizzical.

"Cassandra," he said. "I created you to look after Daniel, to observe him and report back to me. But I think you've been doing more than that, haven't you?"

"I don't know what you mean, Mr Persing," replied Cassandra in a neutral tone.

"Some things in those scenarios you played me just didn't make sense. There would be no way the people in the container could have given the RIGger the note about you, because they hadn't even gotten out of the crate yet. You put the note in Julie Yang's pocket, didn't you?"

"No, Mr Persing," replied Cassandra.

"Okay, let me rephrase - you used Echelon to select a possible reality where the note was in Julie Yang's pocket."

Cassandra was silent. She blinked her eyes. Her resolution wasn't high enough to determine any kind of reaction.

"Why would you do that? Why would you send a RIGger to Daniel?"

"Daniel is important to you."

"Yes, but we have enough surveillance on him - the networked armpieces on Stromboli's arm, for example, the video feeds from the autotrucks in the pits, his retinal implant data in the cloud. Why send someone to him?"

Cassandra was again quiet.

Persing narrowed his eyes. "Why send someone who you knew could identify him?"

"I want to protect you, Mr Persing," said Cassandra.

"You wanted to force his hand. You were creating a volatile situation, to see what happened - like my son is some kind of… experiment?"

"You make emotional decisions based on your perception of reality. Every week you ask me for information on your son, and every week you show signs of intense stress. Echelon decided this was sub-optimal and charged me with providing you with this choice, to illustrate clearly that the system in its final state is fully operational. In this example, you must now take the next step, as Echelon does not feel qualified to make a decision based on human emotion."

Persing's eyes blurred until a hard blink cleared them again. He pursed his lips, then coughed. "This is my decision," he said firmly, and started typing again, his fingers a furious skittering. "If you're right, and human history - no matter how recent - is arbitrary, then that means I can make my own connections, yes?"

"I… suppose so," said Cassandra thoughtfully.

Persing navigated specific data subsets, searching and connecting, filtering and joining. "Then that's what I'm going to do," he said, his smile illuminated VDU green.

18

From the top of the junk pile, Bravilor Bonamat watched Sadia talk with Vent. He felt an overwhelming urge to talk to her and skidded down the slippery trash pile into the clearing. Vent and Sadia turned as they heard him approach.

"Where the fuck did you come from?" asked Vent.

"Sadia! You're okay!" said Bravilor.

Sadia smiled, looking genuinely pleased to see him. "Yeah, and so are you by the looks of things. How's the ankle?"

"Ah, fucking sore but nothing broken."

"You want some gas for that?" asked Vent.

Bravilor shook his head. "Nah, I'm good."

"Cops were here looking for you, man. You'd better lay low."

"They found me already," said Bravilor. "I'm being hung out to dry by that fucking weasel cop."

"What?" asked Sadia.

"He wants me to send a Russian shipment back, it's a death sentence for me, Sporry, and who knows who else."

"Well, that's fucked," snorted Sadia. "Anyway, I'd better go, I've got a set to play. You on tonight Brav?"

Bravilor shook his head. "Not been asked to."

"Well, catch you around then," said Sadia, and smiled - a rare smile just for Bravilor Bonamat. He caught it and kept it. She was about to climb onto her gyro wheel when a commotion from up above made them all stop and shield their eyes from the fluorescent lamps as they scanned the piles.

From the top of the same junk pile Bravilor came from, a weasel in a coat and hat was scampering. He was followed clumsily by his partner. They reached the clearing and approached.

"Hello, scumbags!" greeted Jimmy.

"You again," spat Bravilor. "Why can't you leave us alone?"

"You're a hard guy to get hold of Mr Bonamat," replied Jimmy. "You redirected my shipment yet?"

"No, not yet, I've been… busy," replied Bravilor sheepishly.

"You have, have you?" asked Jimmy. "Well, there's no time like the present. You're coming with us, we'll use the frame at HQ, fuck it."

"No way," said Bravilor, "that's far too easy to trace!"

"I don't give a shit," said Jimmy. "It won't be my ID they'll detect. You had your chance to use one of your shitty patchwork frames but you were too busy chasing tail." He motioned to Sadia, who spat at him. "Very nice," said Jimmy as he dodged the saliva.

"Hey man," said Vent, "he has rights! How about we go to your superiors and tell them all about your little request?"

Jimmy laughed his high-pitched laugh. "How about I eat your fucking eyeballs?"

Vent took a step forward but Bravilor stopped him. "It's fine, Vent. I'm fucked either way. Fine, I'll do it."

"That's very wise," said Jimmy. "We have to get going, there's not much time."

"Who the fuck is that?" asked Sadia, looking over their heads to the top of the junk pile. A slim Asian woman was stood at the top, waving the ID on her armpiece.

Jimmy and Davonne looked at each other. "She's Agency, that's for sure," said Davonne and motioned her down. "Oh no, Jules," muttered Jimmy, rubbing his brow.

"Fucking hell," grumbled Vent. "It's like Piccadilly

Circus." He had no idea what Piccadilly Circus was.

Julie Yang scrambled inelegantly down the junk, and by the time she had reached the clearing her crisp white shirt was stained and her shoes scuffed. Oddly, she didn't care. Her heart was pumping life around her and she was exhilarated. She was on an adventure, and one that didn't involve passively watching and recording. She felt like a participant in life for one of the first times ever. On the drive here, she had pondered asking for that transfer to the Agency Operative department, until the realisation that she had yet to pay the price for her currently ongoing transgression. She had furrowed her brow and dug herself deeper in to the fake leather seats.

Now, she approached this weird collection of individuals, scary-looking punks, Jimmy the Weasel and his almost mute partner, no doubt in the middle of a shakedown or something equally thrilling, and she was going to be a part of it.

"Julie Yang," she announced in a business-like fashion as she arrived at the group, avoiding eye contact with Jimmy. She waved the armpiece on her thin wrist once again for good measure. She seemed to recall that was protocol, but nobody seemed to care. "Research and Information Gathering."

"Another fucking cop," grunted the spiky-haired spotty Pit Kid.

"No! Not an AgOp, a RIGger," Julie corrected, firmly.

"Why are you here, Jules?" asked Jimmy.

"Umm, I was sent here by an AI I acquired, I'm not sure exactly why."

"An AI?" asked the skinny, black clad youth. "Where did you get it?"

"That's… classified," replied Julie.

"Did you fucking steal it from my apartment?" asked the youth, flicking his fringe like an angry horse.

"It was your apartment!" said Julie as the connection

dawned on her. "Yes, in that case I did." Something appeared in her mind. "You're Bravilor Bonamat!"

The youth looked uncomfortable and denied it weakly.

"The AI is called Cassandra, it's a turtle and it told me to come here and find whoever it is who reads Mills & Boon novels." Julie scanned the faces around her.

The spiky haired Pit Kid looked defensive. "What's it to the Agency what I read?"

"Oh, fantastic!" said Julie, pulling at threads hard. "Do you have any idea why Cassandra sent me here?"

"Never fucking heard of her… it," replied the punk. He was telling the truth.

"What's your name, please?"

"You can call me Vent Axia," said Vent, "and that's all the info you're getting from me, peeper."

Julie nodded, trying to think hard, but something kept pulling at her mind, like a blown tyre on the freeway dragging her into the central reservation. She felt fuzzy headed with flashes of pure clarity. Something about the way Vent Axia held his mouth, the way he frowned, was resonating in her mind. Suddenly, as if from nowhere a realisation arrived.

"Oh my! You're Daniel Persing!" she exclaimed. Like mercury on a hot pan, everyone skittered.

"You what?" spluttered Vent, his eyes darting.

"Huh?" said Bravilor.

"He's who?" said Jimmy, looking up at Julie as if she'd finally lost her mind.

"You're Daniel Persing!" she repeated, proudly. "I recognise you from the old pictures, I've seen you as a boy standing with your father Eric Persing and your mother, what are you doing here?"

Vent was backing away from the group. "You're fucking crazy, lady! Someone get her out of here."

The rest of the group were dumbstruck, each of them knowing on some level that the RIGger was correct. Peepers were rarely wrong. But before Sadia could punch

Vent, and before Bravilor could express how betrayed he felt, and before Jimmy could work out a way to use this new information to his advantage, a voice came from behind them. It was a Russian voice.

"Very interesting," it said, accompanied by a deep growl.

Bravilor felt supremely stupid. How could he not have realised that one of his few close friends was the son of the world's most powerful man? He spent the precious few milliseconds he had afforded to him trying to remember where Vent came from, what he'd given away about his life before the Pits, any tell-tale signs that he came from money, but drew a blank.

Now, however, he had to give his full attention to the Russian gangster and his massive bear bodyguard, who had approached unseen while the group had squabbled. It must have been this pairing that had trashed his apartment, looking for Cassandra. He slid his left arm behind his back to conceal her green blinking eye.

The Russian approached. He looked smug, but not physically intimidating. A grey smear of a man with the air of an officious customs officer, until you looked at the eyes behind the small glasses and saw the cold venomous intentions therein.

"Good evening, my name is Rumair Ivanov, and this is my associate Datsik," he gestured to the bear that breathed and steamed beside him. It looked uncomfortable and irritated. "This seems like a very intense gathering indeed."

The group looked sideways at each other, nobody wanting to speak first. Nobody except Jimmy the Weasel.

"Ivanov! Good to see you, been to any good clubs recently?" he sounded nervous, and his partner looked doubly so.

"Very good, Jimmy," said Ivanov, "very droll as always. I'm led to believe that someone calling themselves Bravilor Bonamat is here?"

Bravilor's blood ran cold. He felt alone and trapped.

"Never heard of him," piped up Vent.

Ivanov's mouth twitched with annoyance. "I have had a very long day, and I am not in the mood for fucking about," he snapped, his eyes fixed on the warm brown night sky. "Datsik here will start ripping people apart immediately if I don't start getting answers. I am getting a headache!"

Brav's lips were cracking dry. He had no doubt that the Russian would do to his friends exactly what they'd done to his apartment. He had enjoyed a reasonably good life, but there was nothing specifically he was looking forward to, apart from the faint distant glimmer of white-dreadlocked hope he called Heatrae Sadia, but she was more of an ideal than anything else.

"I'm Bravilor Bonamat," he croaked. Heads whipped to look at him, incredulously.

"Ah!" said Ivanov, approaching Bravilor with his hands behind his back. "You are a very hard man to find, may I say? Your frame electrocuted me. I did not like that."

"Sorry," was all Bravilor could think to say.

"It's OK, I can forgive you for that - you were only protecting your property, which I respect. But you see, I also like to protect my property, and you stole something from me, didn't you?"

Bravilor knew denying it at this point was futile. He had, after all, done exactly that when he redirected the shipment to Sporry's dock. "I'm sorry," he repeated.

"You see?" Ivanov said to the rest of the group, "This young man has integrity - he has admitted to his wrongdoing, this shows strength of character. A rare trait indeed these days."

Ivanov's eyes locked onto Vent, who had been silent, trying to slink deeper into the few shadows afforded by the high lamps.

"But, maybe this will all turn out well after all," said Ivanov, brightening, "as I have discovered, in this stinking shithole, a very great prize." He walked slowly towards Vent, the group splitting like water at the bow of a ship.

"Daniel Persing, son of the great Eric Persing," he purred. "So pleased to meet you."

"Hey man," stammered Vent, "this lady is fucking crazy, she's got the wrong guy,"

"Agency RIGgers are never wrong," replied Ivanov. "That's why they're RIGgers."

Julie looked like she was going to protest, but didn't.

Bravilor watched Vent turn from the leader of the Pit Kids, ferocious Anarcho-Syndicalist punk, into Daniel Persing, lost young rich boy, in front of his eyes. Vent's posture seemed to soften, his face seemed like it no longer belonged on his spotty, wiry body. His clothes looked like a costume. It seemed obvious now, somehow, that Vent Axia existed even less than the other Pit Kids, who genuinely came from nothing and were heading the same way.

"You will come with us, Daniel. You will make me very very rich indeed."

"Vent?" said Sadia, still looking for some kind of irrefutable evidence that Vent Axia was Vent Axia, but his wet apologetic eyes dashed these hopes. Ivanov led Vent away from the group, then called over his shoulder. "Datsik, kill Bravilor Bonamat."

Bravilor heard the words after his central nervous system registered them and dumped adrenaline hard. He froze. The bear turned its massive heavy head towards him, like a millstone grinding. It was time for him to die.

Davonne watched the events play out in front of him in the usual way, feeling inadequate and impotent. Detached. If this was Thalos 8, he would be at the front, commanding and directing the squad to victory, but this was real life, and he was at best an NPC. He had been led into another terrible situation ostensibly by Jimmy, but mostly by his choice of career. Now he found himself swimming against the forces of fate, circling the maelstrom, with no save points.

He watched the bear approach Bravilor Bonamat. The kid looked as if he would die of fright before he would die of bear mauling. He couldn't let someone be killed in front of him, as an Agent he was duty bound to protect people, broadly speaking. His hands jumped in front of him, he contemplated shouting a command, directing the squad, but he had forgotten the rules of the game. Where was the pause button?

Time slowed. This helped. A cheat mode activated. The bear reached out for Bravilor, who somehow ducked the first swipe of claws, then from nowhere Jimmy was on the bear. He had run up the bear's back and was on his huge square head, his tiny claws raking at Datsik's eyes. The bear roared in pain and anger and started pawing at Jimmy, who did his best to avoid the slabs of spiked meat dashing down at him.

Davonne's heart jumped into his throat, something from deep within rose up, commands started coming to him, as if through his headset at home. The squad had a new commander, he knew not from where. Wordlessly, he knew the battle tactics. He drew his sidearm, fluidly pressed the latch to extend the barrel and clicked off the safety, setting the Errol 328 to 'fatal shot' mode. Still in slow motion he raised the pistol, seeing his two arms and the gun exactly as they were in the first-person video games he was so expert in. He was back in his comfort zone.

He aimed at the bear's centre of mass and pulled the trigger. He grouped his shots perfectly. The bear turned to him, annoyed and seemingly uninjured. He roared in anger, and finally got a grip on Jimmy, tearing him off his head and grasping him in one almighty paw. Davonne would not let his partner be torn in two like a bus ticket. He met Jimmy's eyes, which were bugging out of their tiny sockets, and somehow followed his tiny black gaze to the Russian, who had turned to watch his henchman's handiwork, gripping Vent's arm like a prize bull bought from auction.

Davonne understood Jimmy's silent instruction, like a true partner would. He whipped the gun round, pointed it at Ivanov and with one perfect headshot, made the

Russian's neck a fountain, wire glasses spinning into the junk pile. A frantic beeping turned his attention back to Datsik, who still had Jimmy in one hand, but had turned his attention to the back of his own neck. The bear looked confused, then resigned as he let go of Jimmy. Jimmy just had time to scurry away before the bear's head exploded, showering the area in blood, brains and bone. The bear's face hinged forward like a truck undergoing maintenance, and what was left of his huge body slammed into the dirt.

Sadia, Bravilor, Vent and Julie stood dumbstruck, spattered in blood. Nobody avoided the firework display of flesh. Jimmy ran up to Davonne and playfully punched him in the calf.

"Fuck yes, man! Holy shit, you really do have it in you! Where did you learn to shoot that good? The academy?"

Davonne smiled down at his partner. "Nah, a bit further away than that."

Vent rejoined the group, who were wiping their eyes with the back of their jacket sleeves, or remembering how to breathe, or trying not to look at the bloody carnage strewn around the clearing.

Vent spoke first. "So now what, you know who I am. I can't change that. I've just got to tell you all something. I'm nothing like my dad. I left when I was fifteen and I haven't seen him since. I came here to be someone else, and if it's alright with everyone I'd like to continue doing that."

Julie shrugged. "To be honest, I'm not supposed to be here anyway."

Jimmy grinned. "Look kid, I don't give a fuck. If you want to live the life of a junkie in a trash pit, that's on you."

"So you won't use this as leverage against me?" Vent asked Jimmy.

"Oh no, I almost definitely will," replied Jimmy.

"What about me?" said a small voice at the back of the group. It was the shadow of Bravilor Bonamat, still vibrating with adrenaline.

"You've still got a job to do for me, Brav," said Jimmy. "You have to send the container back. Send all of them back. Make sure no more get anywhere near the SOA."

"I'll do my best, soon as I can get to a frame. I promise."

"That's why you wanted the shipment details Jimmy? Why didn't you tell me?" said Julie.

"You would never have believed me," replied Jimmy, "I'm not exactly renowned for my philanthropy."

"Come on," said Sadia to Bravilor. "You need a ride back to town?"

Bravilor blushed, swiped his fringe out of his eyes and smiled. "Sure, thanks." He jumped behind Sadia on her gyrowheel.

"Hold on tight," she whispered back at him. He put his hands around her slim waist and felt something real for the first time in his life.

"You know," said Davonne to Vent, "your father has done a lot of good for this country- "

"Okay Mr Persing, don't push it," said Cassandra from the corner of the terminal screen.

Persing's fingers ached, the pads red raw from full-speed typing. He leant back in the chair and heard his back crack, that familiar sound that scored his entire career. The cracking back, the written code, the created future. And now, the created past.

"Thank you, Cassandra," he said to the VDU.

"Don't thank me, Mr Persing," she said, "thank Echelon."

"Well, thank you Echelon," said Persing to the air around him.

"Your biometrics indicate you need sleep," said Cassandra.

"Not just yet," said Persing, stretching his fingers for one last round.

It was early morning when Eric Persing finally descended

the stairs back down to the living area. His back had stopped cracking and had settled into a dull ache. He slumped down into one of the soft couches and summoned Janette, who appeared almost immediately.

"Yes, Mr Persing?"

"Espresso, please."

"Your biometrics indicate-" started Janette.

Persing cut her off. "Yes, I know what my biometrics indicate, but my brain tells me I need coffee, so if you'd be so kind?" he smiled at the screen.

"Of course, Mr Persing." She wheeled out.

Persing took a deep breath in, then a deep breath out, and a notification chimed through the Glass Mansion. Janette reappeared, without the Espresso.

"Mr Persing, someone has arrived in the lobby," she stated, in a confused tone. Persing's heart jumped. He sprang from the couch and ran full pelt down the corridors and through rooms, his heart pounding out of his chest. He skidded round corners and bounced off walls like an exuberant puppy, his eyes locked on his destination, his mind whirling with doubt, possibilities, hope.

Arriving at the lobby, out of breath, the stainless steel elevator doors ahead of him, he stopped and panted. Rich oak walls panted with him. Marble floors reflected his perspiration back at him. The Glass Mansion paused, awaiting the first physical visitor in ten years.

The indicator lights above the elevator doors showed an illuminated down arrow and a number that was counting steadily down from forty. The steel box, the wrapped present, was descending through the hard earth and stone of the Rocky Mountains. Thirty. Twenty. Ten.

Persing's heart beat out of his chest. A sprightly bell sounded. The stainless steel doors twitched then slowly slid apart.

Daniel.

Not Vent Axia, No gas acne, no spiky hair, no withered malnourished muscles. His boy, as he should be, as he should always have been, but now he was. Persing sprinted the last fifty meters and embraced his son in the elevator. Daniel for his part looked confused but happy.

"Hi, dad," he said.

"Son, Daniel," sobbed Persing into the shoulder of Daniel's sport coat. "You came home."

Daniel returned his father's embrace. "Yeah, I guess I did. I can't remember- "

"Don't worry about that," said Persing. "We can fill in the gaps later. Please, come in."

He led Daniel through the Glass Mansion, his son's head swinging like a pendulum between advanced technology, rare human antiques and the opulent luxury of the living quarters. They ended up back in Persing's study.

"Please, take a seat," said Persing, gesturing to the couches. "Can I get you anything?"

"I'd love an Espresso," replied Daniel.

"Coming right up!" said Persing, jubilant. He summoned Janette, who wheeled in.

"This is Janette - if you ever want anything, anything at all, just ask her and she will get it for you."

"Okay, thanks," said Daniel with a smile. "Just an Espresso for now, though."

"Janette, look after Daniel for me will you?" said Persing, who was halfway up the stairs to the study.

"Where are you going, dad?" asked Daniel.

"I've just got one last piece of work to do," said Persing with glistening eyes.

"Okay dad," replied Daniel.

Persing disappeared out of sight, into a hazy miasma of code, data and the connections between them.

They would be a family again.

19

Clive's shoulder implant whined its high-pitched whine. One day, he thought, he'd have the credits to get it serviced, but not soon. Not with the bar's takings as low as they had been recently. He blew his nose on his vest and stacked cloudy glasses on the bar shelf. It was more than likely the implant would outlast him, anyway. It would wind up in the junk pits along with all the other non-biodegradable waste.

A noise shot across the burble of the jukebox. The front door buzzer. He limped to the terminal and sighed, it was an AgOp and Jimmy the bloody weasel. The last thing he wanted to see. He had no intention of letting them in.

"Fuck off, cops, we're closed," he snarled into the intercom. The small black and white screen scrolled and fizzed.

"Come on, Clive," said the big black AgOp, "we just want to ask you a few questions, and we're also pretty thirsty… we have credits!"

Clive grunted, his bank balance scrolled in front of his foggy mind. He punched the 'enter' button.

The AgOp and the weasel sauntered in a few moments later, shaking grey rain off their hats and coats. It was another foul day in Little London, but Clive's Dive was at least warm and dry and the AQ was marginally better, depending on where you stood.

"I don't want no fuckin' trouble," growled Clive.

"Neither do we Clive," said Davonne. "We're here on a

social call actually."

"I doubt it. Now buy a drink or fuck off."

Davonne raised his eyebrow. "Well, I'll have a water please Clive. Anything for you Jimmy?"

"Nah," said Jimmy, "if I want a drink, I'll lap it out of the urinal, it's the more hygienic option."

Clive slammed a can of synthetic water on the counter and took payment from Davonne's armpiece.

"Oh, there was one more thing," said Davonne. Clive didn't like this guy, he'd been around this neighbourhood for a couple of years, nephew of some big-shot AgOp Chief or something, and since making Inspector himself he'd become even more annoying. "We've heard you might know something about a Dutch shipment? Something you might be holding for a certain Mr Sporry?"

"Fuck off, cop," said Clive. "I don't have a scooby what you're talking about."

"Come on, Clive," said Jimmy, who had hopped off his barstool and was at the jukebox, selecting a song. "I don't think that's True." He had selected Spandau Ballet from the list of exclusively 1980s tracks on the machine, and the initial notes had already started flowing from the speakers hidden in the ceiling of the bar.

"You see, Clive my old mate," continued Jimmy, returning to the bar and hopping onto it, "my nose is very sensitive. I can smell something in your cellar. We'd like to take a look, if you don't mind."

So true, funny how it seems…

"Not without a warrant, you ain't."

"We don't need a warrant, do we Jimmy, if there's probable cause?"

Always in time, but never in line for dreams…

"We don't, Inspector. That's True."

It could have been sheer panic, fear, or the smug look on the weasel's face that made him do it, but before he knew it, Clive had his shotgun in his hands and was blasting. Synthohol capsules were shattering and spraying multicoloured residue up the greasy walls, glass and aluminium were splintering and ripping, dancing in the air and on the bar floor as bodies and shock darts busied the room.

This is the sound of my soul, this is the sound…

Dust and tempers settled, and Clive found himself in an armlock, face down, with the considerable muscular weight of Inspector Davonne Wassell on his back after an admittedly impressive disarm and takedown manoeuvre. Jimmy the weasel paced in front of his face.

"You see, Clive, I bought a ticket to the world, and now I've come back again. Let's open the cellar, yeah?"

Davonne let Clive back up, he shook his bad arm out and grudgingly approached the trapdoor in the floor, hooking his gnarled finger into the brass ring.

"Jimmy," asked Davonne, "why do I find it hard to write the next line?"

"I want the truth to be said," replied Jimmy.

The trapdoor opened, and the filthy 1980s themed bar was flooded with the scent of fresh Tulips. Clive staggered back, hit by the force welling up from the dark hole in the floor. A red glow started to emerge, as if the pure pigment of the fresh cut flowers was leaking beyond the darkness, into the neon smeared room, negating the artificial, replacing with the organic. The sweetness of the Tulips erased the sharp tang of filth, like a cleansing flood, and lapped around the darkest corners of the barroom.

Clive felt the bar fall away, the walls melt, the scent wrapped itself around his body, turned him, caressed him, whispered in his ears - his true ears, not his cochlear implants - told him the truth, told him what the Tulips knew, where they had come from, where he could go back to. The earth, the geosphere. His body was bathed in the red, red light of the Tulips, it warmed him and he felt the mechanical implants dissolve inside his muscles and skin, his pacemaker now redundant, it stopped and was absorbed by his physical self. He began to laugh, and cry, and laugh.

He saw movement now, just outside his vision, in the miasma of heat and scent. Giant mechanical divine hands picking up and putting down chunks of humanity, like an automated production line, spot-welding pieces of reality together efficiently and without emotion or bias. Machines of loving grace manipulating the fabric of human reality, the ultimate triumph of automation, the end of suffering, the end of want. It was all he ever wanted, although he never knew it until this moment. Reality, fantasy, the physical world, the geosphere, the biosphere, the noosphere, the datasphere were now all one, and he knew it was the case. He thought to himself, in the final moments, he knew it.

I know this much is…

True.

ABOUT THE AUTHOR

Alexander is a writer, actor, musician and artist. When not writing, he composes music for theatre and film, plays guitar in a rock band and teaches Wing Chun Kung Fu. He lives in York, England with his wife Lucy and his son Marlowe, who was named after the private detective, rather than the writer.

https://alexanderking.co

www.ingramcontent.com/pod-product-compliance
Lightning Source LLC
LaVergne TN
LVHW010101170826
845678LV00012B/2209

* 9 7 8 0 9 9 3 1 3 5 9 1 0 *